'Sam Millar's Karl Kane series is one of the high points in crime writing today. Millar can string words together like diamonds on a necklace and craft a hell of a good tale, but Kane, his protagonist, is what makes the series a gem. Childhood trauma damaged him so severely that it was like a napalm strike on his psyche. Kane is kind to his friends, a blight on those who threaten the people he cares about. Kane is the kind of guy you'd call up for a beer and a good chat, or if you needed help dumping the body of the guy you just shot in the head. Who could ask for more? Totally addictive and brilliant.'

James Thompson, international bestselling author, *Snow Angels* and the *Inspector Kari Vaara* series.

'If Charles Dickens were a thriller writer, *Past Darkness* would be his masterpiece. But Sam Millar beat him to it with his latest can't put down Karl Kane noir thriller. Millar's acclaimed descriptive powers once again fashion some of fiction's darkest characters, ones your soul wishes did not exist even though your mind knows are out there. *Past Darkness* is another winner from the very gifted Millar.'

Jeffrey Siger, international bestselling author, *Sons of Sparta*

'Karl is Everyman, forever walking wide-eyed into trouble but always managing to avoid disaster. In previous books Karl merely faced death. In *Past Darkness* he also has to face down the horrors of his own childhood. A grisly tale grippingly told by an author whose words burrow down into the most squeamish parts of our psyche.'

John McAllister, critically acclaimed author, *The Station Sergeant* and *Barlow by the Book*

Winner of many awards, including the Brian Moore Award for Short Stories, and the Aisling Award for Art and Culture, Sam Millar is the author of highly acclaimed crime novels, several of which have sold internationally. He has also written a bestselling memoir, *On the Brinks*.

'Millar's words will mesmerize you. He is like a poet of darkness...'
Village Voice, New York

Also by Sam Millar

Fiction
The Darkness of Bones
Dark Souls
The Redemption Factory
Black's Creek

Karl Kane novels
Bloodstorm
The Dark Place
Dead of Winter

Memoir
On the Brinks

Play
Brothers in Arms

Recipient *Golden Balais d'or* for Best Crime Book of 2013–14
Recipient *Trophées 813, du meilleur roman*
Le Monde's prestigious Top Twenty Thrillers for 2013-2014
   for *Bloodstorm: A Karl Kane Novel*

www.millarcrime.com

PAST
DARKNESS

SAM MILLAR

PAST DARKNESS

A KARL KANE NOVEL

BRANDON

First published 2015 by
Brandon
An imprint of The O'Brien Press Ltd
12 Terenure Road East, Rathgar,
Dublin 6, Ireland.

Tel: +353 1 4923333; Fax: +353 1 4922777
E-mail: books@obrien.ie.

Website: www.obrien.ie

ISBN: 978-1-84717-741-4

Cover image: Getty Images

1 3 5 7 6 4 2
15 17 19 18 16

Printed and bound by Nørhaven, Denmark.
The paper used in this book is produced using pulp from managed forests.

DEDICATION

Past Darkness is dedicated to two great friends. Steve McDonagh, my original publisher of the Kane books, for giving me the idea to write a series of novels based on a Belfast PI. And best-selling American crime writer, Jim Thompson, who died so tragically and so young, and an inspiration to me. Both friends stood by me through thick and thin, never giving up on me, even when I wanted to. Always remembered.

ACKNOWLEDGEMENTS

A special thank-you to all the crew at The O'Brien Press, especially Eoin O'Brien for his patience and dedication to *Past Darkness*.

Prologue

Did you ever have to find a way to survive and you knew your choices were bad? Irving Rosenfeld, *American Hustle*

Dark thunderclouds hung low over the fortress-like building on the outskirts of south Belfast. Trussed up with razor wire and security cameras, the bleak, pre-war institution looked more like a medieval prison than a place supposedly dedicated to the care of rebellious children.

The administration liked to boast that the grim walls were there to keep bad people out, and to protect the building's adolescent inhabitants, and that God's work was being done within.

The boast was a running joke among the staff…

Pastor William Kilkee appeared out of breath as he stepped from the tiny room into the narrow, dimly lit corridor. His wrinkled brow was newly damp with sweat, and his upper lip glistened like a snail-trail on a garden stone.

He looked up and down the corridor, nervously adjusting the dog collar resting on the folds of his skinny neck. Adjusted his fly. Subconsciously ran his bony fingers through the sea of thick grey hair atop his large skull, before proceeding cautiously up the corridor.

The lateness of the hour seemed amplified by the wooden ticking of a large grandfather clock standing like a sentinel in the centre of the grand hall, near the end of the corridor.

Tick, tick, tick, tick, tick…

He approached the grand hall, the ticking becoming louder, more insistent. It unnerved him slightly, though he made the same journey continually, night after night, in adventures filled with sodomy, rape and cruelty.

Loud thunderclaps sent silvery blue light careering around the dark corridor, unsettling him even more. He hated stormy nights, wind and rain, especially thunder and lightning. They put him in mind of the god he had abandoned a long time ago, and how, one day, he would have to answer for all his depraved deeds to that same forsaken god.

He stopped. Glanced behind. Looked deep into the corridor's sombre greyness. Thought he saw a chalky figure, way off in the distant haze. He wanted to shout out, *who's there?*, but feared he would betray his nocturnal transgressions.

Tick, tick, tick, tick, tick…

Just about to move off, his ears picked up the sound more acutely. It wasn't the sound of the great clock he was hearing, but something else, something more sinister. Not tick, tick. But…

Click, click, click, click, click…

He moved quickly down the corridor, almost at a trot.

His room was at the end of the hallway, a few seconds away. Safe harbour.

Click, click, click, click, click…

The clicking was becoming louder. It had attached itself to the inside of his skull. Tapping on it, *tap, tap, tap, tap,* like some tormented woodpecker.

Click, click, click, click, click…

He fumbled for his key. Inserted it into the door. Practically fell into the room, slamming the door too loudly behind him.

For the longest time, all he could hear was the sound of his laboured breathing ghosting in the room.

Knock-knock!

The knock on the door frayed what little nerve he had left.

Knock-knock! More insistent this time.

He crept to the door, and peeped out through the spyhole.

She was standing there, naked, in all her fleshy glory, smiling that sweet, innocent smile of seduction and want.

His saggy cock moved, stirred from its slumber.

'*No, not tonight…*' he finally managed to whisper, through the closed door. '*Too dangerous.*'

'But you like danger, Pastor. You always said it keeps you young, keeps your cock fit.'

He felt his face redden at the coarseness of her words, even though she spoke the truth.

'Tomorrow night. We'll–'

'I can lick all wee Rhonda's juice from that big cock of yours.

I saw you leaving her room, back there. I bet you haven't dried it off yet?' She made a slurping sound at the side of the door. '*Hmm. Yummy.* You'd like that, wouldn't you, having Mister Cocky all nice and dry?'

He felt faint with lust and desire. His knees were trembling, threatening to buckle. He leaned his back against the door, as if fearful she would get in. He closed his eyes, but she was there still, in the leathery under-garment of his lids, all wet and ready.

With his back still tight against the door, he turned the door handle, then stepped away.

The door slowly opened. She stood there, smiling. Two knitting needles in her hands, drumming them off each other.

Click, click, click, click, click…

'What…why've you knitting needles in your– *aghhhhhhhhhhhhhhhhhhhhhh!*'

She reached up quickly, then applied pressure, squeezing the needles down into his eyes, twisting and turning them with delighted satisfaction.

He staggered back, blood oozing from each eyeball in spurting hiccups. Instinctively, he tried to pull the needles out, but despite her smallness, she was too strong for him, her youthfulness forcing his ageing body onto his knees. A matador grounding a bull.

The needles journeyed onwards, tunnelling their way through rock-bone and pliable meat. With a final thrust of her wrists, the needles pierced his brain in a brutal yet elegant *coup de grâce*.

She kicked the door shut. Sat down on his favourite chair. With a mild curiosity, she watched his death-knell spasms on the ground, as he intoned the help of God, Satan, any other underworld creatures roaming the bloody twilight. His mouth was filling with blood, forcing him to splutter and gag, as if drowning underwater.

It was over in less than ten minutes. Despite the satisfaction of ringing in his death, she felt robbed. All those long years of abuse for ten minutes of pain – it seemed small change in the pocket of justice. She sincerely wished for the power to bring him back from the dead, so that she could kill him again, over and over.

She fled the room, twenty minutes later, hoping never to see that terrible place again. That was when the alarms rang out…

Chapter One

He was a ferocious man. He had been ill-made in the making. He had not been born right, and he had not been helped any by the moulding he had received at the hands of society. The hands of society are harsh, and this man was a striking sample of its handiwork. Jack London, *White Fang*

A nondescript van pulled up outside the tumbling walls surrounding the large Victorian house. The neglected building, in an isolated village on the outskirts of Belfast, was camouflaged in night shadows and overhanging leafage.

The van remained parked for what seemed an eternity. Eventually, a man squeezed his body from the driving seat, stepping out into the crisp, cool air.

No ordinary man. Fearsome in many ways. Unnatural in size and appearance, as if built by some devious god of deception and devilment. His face was a eulogy of darkness and revulsion, a death-shroud of disfigurement. A large, deep scar shaped like a 'Z' trenched his face.

He walked to the high, rusted gates, and pushed them open without exertion. The great house came fully into view like a pop-up book, making him smile like an eager child at Christmas discovering boxes of wonderment, dark and mysterious.

The house had seen better years, swamped by luxuriant weeds and brambles. Stocky, mangled trees cast twitching iron shadows over the structure. Paint had long vanished from its pockmarked wooden skin, and most of the windows had been destroyed by the elements and time, giving it a Poesque air.

After a long moment of breathing in his surroundings, he returned to the van, swinging it in from the roadside, away from prying eyes. Moving steadily, he began to unload some items stocked inside, paying particular attention to a large, heavy rug rolled up in the back.

He lifted the rug easily, shipped it upon one powerful shoulder, and walked casually towards the house. He opened the front door with his free hand, and stepped in. Musty smells of remembrance, redolent of a lover's perfume, greeted him.

Closing his eyes, he sucked in the smells deeply, his massive chest bellowing in and out. When his eyelids lifted, tears were welling in the brims.

A lost child finally found…

He stood in silent contemplation under the doorway's arch for some moments, before stepping in and closing the impressive oak door behind him. The three heavy bolts slid home into their niches.

Energised now, he began to climb the bare, creaky stairs, taking them two at a time, his speedy stride surprising for a man of such bulk. He barely seemed to notice the massive rug resting on his shoulder, so fluent were his movements and strength.

He reached the third floor, halting outside the one-time master bedroom. Easing the rug down outside the door, he entered the room, his eyes focusing on the centre of the bare floor. A reddened patch, faded by time into a ghostly stain. He knelt down, ran his hands over the stain, feeling something coursing darkly throughout his body; something long dead, now given renewed existence, like Victor Frankenstein granting life to his Monster.

He stood, and began discarding all clothing, despite the cold night air coming freely in through the many gaps in the house. Fully exposed, his nude body was covered in tattoos of smirking skulls. Only the fully erect penis had escaped the craftsman's ink, making it stand out like a stranger in a strange land.

Out on the landing, the large rug shifted slightly, a tiny, barely visible movement among the shadows. A hand appeared from inside, curled up like a withered flower.

The tiny hand of a child.

Chapter Two

Down these mean streets a man must go who is not himself mean…a common man and yet an unusual man. He talks as the man of his age talks, that is, with rude wit, a lively sense of the grotesque, a disgust for sham, and a contempt for pettiness.
Raymond Chandler, *The Simple Art of Murder*

Karl Kane's mobile began ringing on the bedroom table, just as the pills he had consumed four hours earlier were starting to lose their cosy effectiveness. He could tell it was early morning because of the particular quietness seeping in from the surrounding streets: no sounds of drunken louts or screaming teenagers spilling out from nearby pubs and clubs in and around Hill Street in Belfast's trendy Cathedral Quarter.

In a way, he was grateful for the phone's shrill insistence. He had been immersed in another nightmare of drowning in blood – his mother's – but this time it was so intense, he could taste iron clinging to his teeth like broken floss. The nightmares were now a nightly occurrence, increasingly vivid in their madness and malice.

He dreaded going back to sleep.

Karl let the mobile's ringing guide him back to reality for a few more seconds before glancing at the luminous alarm clock on the table. The clock revealed the dangerous side of four in the morning. Troubling phone calls at four in the morning, in Karl's profession as a private investigator, only ever meant one thing: trouble.

Reaching over, he hooked the phone with a finger and thumb before staring at the number on the screen.

'Lipstick…? What the hell?'

'Karl…?' said the groggy voice of Naomi, partner-in-crime and lover, snuggling beside him in the bed. 'Who…who's calling at this time of night?'

Extremely attractive, Naomi was dark-skinned with large hazel eyes and wild black hair. Despite the northern cadence in her voice, it sill commanded a strong trace of the south.

'Sorry, love. Didn't mean to waken you. It's Lipstick.'

'Lipstick…? God, I hope she's not in some sort of trouble?'

'Trouble? Lipstick?' Karl said sarcastically, hitting the button on the mobile. 'Lipstick? What kind of shit are you in now?'

'Karl? What kept you?' Lipstick whispered, edginess in her young voice. *'I've been waiting ages for you to answer.'*

'You have? Please accept my sincere apologies for that. Like most law-abiding citizens, I was in bed, trying to sleep.'

'Say you won't get mad.'

'That's a bit like when someone tells you not to get nervous. The first thing you do is *get* nervous.'

'I need your help. I'm in a lot of trouble.'

'Tell me something new. Where are you?'

'Locked in a bathroom.'

'*What?* What the bloody hell, Lipstick? You call me at four in the morning just to get you out of a–'

'In the Europa.'

'The Europa…?'

'Yes.'

'I take it you're whispering because you can't speak too loud, in case someone hears you.'

'Yes.'

'A disgruntled client?'

'If that means ugly, angry and smelly, then yes. He's screaming through the door right now that he's gonna rape and then kill me. I'm scared, Karl. He means it. He's ramming the door right now. Listen.'

Lipstick must have been holding her mobile near the door. In the background, Karl could here screaming and loud thumps.

'Room number?' Karl quickly swung his legs out of bed, parking his impressive bulk on the edge.

'Fourteen.'

'Has this creep got a name?'

'Calls himself Graham Butler. He's from London, I think. He…he wanted me to do things I hadn't agreed to. He wouldn't pay me for what I'd already done for him, so I took his watch in exchange.'

'I'll be there within five minutes. Hold tight.'

'*Karl?*'

'What?'

'Look tough.'

'At four in the morning and wearing pyjamas?'

Naomi waited until Karl killed the connection.

'What's she got herself into, now?'

'Something I hope to get her out of before I get too deep into.' He quickly put on a pair of socks, while searching for his Samuel Windsor loafers.

'You can't keep putting yourself in danger, every time she calls.'

'Tell me how to say no to the person who saved my life, and I'll do it.'

'Get off the guilt trip. You've repaid her a hundred times. She's ripping the arse clean out of it.'

'I know she is, and it's *my* arse taking the hammering, along with my haemorrhoids. Hopefully, I shouldn't be too long. Go back to sleep.'

He gave Naomi a quick kiss, and headed out the door.

It was raining when Karl arrived outside the Europa four minutes later. Residing a few streets away helped. The filthy rain came down in thick, leach-shaped drops, making a bizarre echoing sound as it hit the top of parked cars. He cursed under his breath for not bringing an umbrella.

He parked his car in a side street, and hurriedly headed towards the front entrance of the hotel.

Bombed over thirty times, the grand old building had earned the unenviable sobriquet of the most bombed hotel in Europe. Or as Belfastians flippantly referred to it: that blasted hotel.

The area was usually buzzing with tourists, but at this time of morning, foot traffic had wisely disappeared, replaced by parcels of nomadic homeless people. Outside the hotel, a fleet of black taxis resembling giant metallic beetles lurked in the shadows, their suspicious-looking drivers assembled like Alfred Hitchcock villains waiting to carry out villainous deeds.

Karl passed through the revolving doors and into the modern and bright reception of the grand foyer. He was immediately eyed by a suspicious young concierge, who looked as if he had yet to tackle his first razor.

'May I help you, *sir*?' the young man said disdainfully, look-ing a dishevelled and drenched Karl up and down.

'No, you're okay, son. Just heading up to see my old school mate Graham – Graham Butler – up in room fourteen.' Karl made a movement towards the lift, but was quickly blocked by the pimply adolescent.

'You can't go up until I call Mister Butler on the phone. That's hotel policy.'

Karl glanced at the young man's name tab: Raymond.

'Hotel policy, Raymond? Is it hotel policy to turn a blind eye to janes and johns?'

Raymond's face reddened. 'I...I don't know what you're talking about.'

'No? I never forget a name. A friend of mine – who just happens to be in trouble right now, as I waste time speaking to you – mentioned a Raymond to me. Likes to have his palms greased for turning a blind eye to illegal nocturnal manoeuvres of the sexual kind.'

'I...I...don't know what that means.'

'No? Okay then, we'll discuss the birds and bees later. Right now, be a good boy and hold that pose. I'll be back down in less than five minutes. No one will be any the wiser. And here, this is for forgetting.' Karl slipped a tenner into Raymond's waistcoat pocket. 'Oh, if I find out you phoned room fourteen, and ruined my surprise, it'll not be your palm I'll be greasing, when I return.'

Raymond, now looking a little faint, moved smoothly out of the way.

Ten seconds later, Karl stepped out of the elevator and immediately took stock outside room fourteen. A muffled but angry voice could be heard as he levelled his ear against the door.

Standing back a good few inches, Karl studied the door. Thought about trying to kick the formidable-looking structure in. Quickly realised the implausibility of such a ridiculous act.

He calmly rang the bell instead.

'Who the fuck is it?' a harsh male voice shouted.

'Room service, sir.'

The door snapped open, revealing a nude, sweating man, covered in tattoos. He was stocky, gym-manufactured, fake-bronzed and had ridiculously white teeth. A big bastard of a brute, he stood six large and six small, and was in his late forties *auditioning* for thirty. His hands were enormous – unlike his diminutive cock. All pubic hairs had been shaven in his private area. Karl shuddered as an image of Kojak sucking his famous lollipop violated his mind.

'What the fuck're you on about, dickhead? I didn't ask for any fucking room service,' Butler snarled, trying to sound like a tough guy in a B-movie.

'Facial masseur, monsieur,' replied the genuine article of tough guy personified.

'I don't need a facial anything–'

Karl's uppercut caught Butler under the jaw so hard, the thug staggered backwards in mid-ride over a sofa, before speedily spreading out in crucifixion formation on the floor, moaning.

'You do now, scumbag.' Quickly walking over to the bathroom, Karl banged on the door. 'Lipstick! Open the hell up! It's me. Karl.'

The door opened a fraction, revealing a young, matchstick-thin girl, in her early twenties. Her features were a prescription of heroin-addiction misery. She was nude, awkwardly trying to cover up her private parts.

'Is…is he gone, Karl?'

'Let's just say he'll be out for a while – what…? What the *hell* happened to your face?'

Lipstick's eyes were turning an angry purple, partially closing. A web of bloody drool dripped from her busted mouth.

'He got angry because I wouldn't do anal for him. You… you know I only do anal for people I like, Karl, don't you?'

Karl made an uncomfortable face. 'I wouldn't let Naomi hear you say it like *that*. She might get the wrong impression. Hurry up and get dressed. I'm taking you to the Mater.'

'But…I don't need to go to the hospital. It's just a few smacks in the gob and–'

'*Do* as I say. I'm not in the mood for negotiations.' Karl turned, walked over to the moaning Butler. 'Hard man, eh? Like picking on defenceless little girls?'

Blood was smearing Butler's mouth. It looked vulgar. Like the Joker in *Batman*.

Smirking, Butler looked up at Karl. 'You…you don't know…who you're fucking with, you and your little whore.'

Karl smiled like a politician on voting day. 'They say you should never kick a man when he's down, but in your case I say, name me a better time?' Karl kicked the smirking face twice, before placing his formidable weight down on Butler's fully exposed bare balls.

'*Fuckkkkkkkkkkkkkkkkkkkkkkkkkkkkkkkkkkkkkkkkk!*' Butler screamed, his hands trying desperately to pull Karl's foot away.

'You don't look so hard now, not where I'm standing, *dickhead.*' Karl applied more pressure.

'*Fuckkkkkkkkkkkkkkkkkkkkkkkkkkkkkkkkkkkkkkkkk!*' Butler's face knotted inwards with pain. He vomited a greenish grey lumpy substance.

'That's enough, Karl!' Lipstick shouted from the bathroom, hurriedly getting dressed. 'No need to hurt him any more.'

But the rage and blood-rush was with Karl, and he continued ball-pressing.

'I said that's enough!' Lipstick ran up to Karl, pulling him away.

'You're too forgiving, kiddo. How many times have I told you to toughen up?'

'Toughen up like you, the biggest softy on the planet? Besides, I got this.' Lipstick dangled an expensive-looking watch in front of Karl's eyes, almost as if trying to hypnotize him. 'He'll hate losing this more than any kicking you can give him. He's that sort of bastard.'

Fatigued, Karl sat down on the overturned sofa, and let out a sigh.

'I'm getting way too old for this kind of shit, kiddo, and you're way too young to be doing the kind of shit *you* do.'

Lipstick put her emaciated arms around Karl's neck and kissed his cheek, leaving her trademark shimmering on his skin.

'I love you, Karl Kane. You know that, don't you?'

'The story of my life. Everyone loves me when they're in trouble.'

'Not like me, they don't,' Lipstick said, with such earnest intensity it was heart-breaking to hear. 'I *love* you.'

Karl quickly untangled her arms from his neck, and began pushing himself up wearily from the sofa, like an old heavy-weight boxer using the ropes for balance.

'C'mon, kiddo. Let's get the hell out of here. We're heading to the Mater.'

'Do…do we really need to go, Karl? They might start asking awkward questions and–' Uncontrollably, Lipstick started giggling.

'What the hell's so funny?'

Lipstick pointed at Karl's legs. 'You really *are* wearing pyjamas.'

Chapter Three

Do not be afraid of what you are about to suffer. I tell you, the devil will put some of you in prison to test you, and you will suffer persecution for ten days. Be faithful, even to the point of death, and I will give you life as your victor's crown.

Revelation, 12:17

The inside of the large house stank of the festering human leakage of urine and excrement, coupled with dampness and the particular flavour of coldness associated with loneliness and despair.

Death, also, in the godless gloom.

Murder, specifically.

Oh such a horrible murder.

The master bedroom remained practically bare, except for the years of yesterday strewn everywhere: old newspapers browning and curling like autumn leaves, and once-happy clothes turned to sad-rags of moth-fodder.

Practically bare, except for the thin, diseased mattress in the middle of the floor, and the young girl's body curved into a foetal position atop the bedding. Her body resembled a straw doll left out in the evening rain for too long. She was adorned in a long, flowery dress from an era long forgotten.

At the entrance to the room, Scarman stood like a medieval giant, naked, muscles framed powerfully in the door. His face was arrogantly chiselled like a great, pale wolf. His eyes were those of the departed, and he focused those dead eyes on the girl.

In the claustrophic darkness, the girl's skin gleamed like a ghostly beacon, more an apparition than something tangible and breathing.

Stalking silently to the mattress, he knelt down and brought his nose close to her, inhaling deeply. A cloying onion odour of unwashed skin filled his nostrils. Coupled with that smell, which never failed to arouse the darkness in him: the smell of the young.

For such a thin little thing, she had struggled gallantly, punching and kicking. But now she was silent and still. As still as fallen snow in the breaking of winter's twilight; so still, he thought she could be dead.

But she wasn't dead. Not yet. Not until *he* was ready. He needed one more to accompany her on the journey ahead. He had been unsuccessful up to now in finding the other special one. The next couple of days, he hoped, would be more fruitful.

He left the room as silently as he had entered, and only then did the girl abandon her pretence, opening the curtains of her eyelids slowly.

Her gaze was filled with caution and weariness, but also something else; something not quite right, carried deep down inside her: a sinister darkening slowly awakening, revealing a provenance of past horrors. Perhaps a warning of terrible things to come; terrible things about to be unleashed into the murderous madness being prepared for those about to die, or those about to kill.

Chapter Four

Act well your part, there all the honour lies.
Alexander Pope, *An Essay on Man*

'Look at the state of you,' Naomi said, placing a steaming cup of coffee barely within arm's reach of the sofa Karl was stretched out on. 'What time did you get in at this morning?'

'About an hour ago,' Karl replied, yawning while supinely reaching for the coffee. Black circles were developing under his bloodshot eyes.

'You'll choke on that if you don't sit up right.'

'Wishful thinking on your behalf.'

'Couldn't you've at least phoned, let me know where you were? I was worried sick when you didn't come back.'

'Is that what's biting the arse off you? You know I left in a hurry. I forgot the damn mobile. Okay? Now, can I drink this coffee before it gets cold?'

Naomi ignored him. Sat down at the breakfast table. Clicked on the digital radio. Leafing through the morning newspaper, she stopped at a small article on page two.

'They still haven't found that wee girl, Tara Kennedy.

Remember? The one who ran away from that foster home, Blackmore, over in south Belfast. It's been almost three months since she went missing.'

'That's why I don't read those rags anymore. Nothing but bad news in them. And you wonder why people living in Belfast are depressed? If its not tablets, it's tabloids they're on.'

Naomi stared sadly at Tara's photo. 'Such a lovely wee thing. It says she's fifteen, but she barely looks ten in this picture.'

'Can you please keep all that grim news to yourself? I don't want to hear about it.'

'Why are you being so ill-tempered this morning? Are your haemorrhoids acting up?'

'No, that's not the *bloody* reason. If you really must know, I've had very little sleep. Been waiting in a sardine-filled emergency room with Lipstick, up in the Mater.'

'Lipstick in the hospital…?' Naomi immediately placed the newspaper back down on the table, looking troubled. 'For heaven's sake, why didn't you say something earlier?'

'You didn't give me time, did you, with your interrogation?'

'I just thought she was looking for some money from you, and you didn't want me to know.'

'That's your suspicious mind working.'

'What happened?'

'A steroid-swollen scumbag beat the crap out of her, over in the Europa. That's what the phone call was about this morning.'

Naomi looked horrified. 'God the night, Karl. Is she okay?'

'Her face looks terrible, but the doctor said she should be fine in a couple of weeks. She's lucky not to be scarred for life.'

'What about the lowlife who did it? Did the police arrest him?'

'How the hell could the cops be brought into it, knowing Lipstick's form? I even had to make up a cock-and-bull story to the nurse in the Mater, who probably thought I was the one who did it. Sitting in the waiting room soaked to the skin and wearing pyjamas didn't help either. The looks I was getting, as if I was some sort of perv.'

'The thug got away, then?'

Karl made a grunting sound. 'Let's just say I had a ball of a time with what little balls he had to boast about. By now, though, they've swollen to the size of Space Hoppers. He'll be pissing glass for weeks, hopefully. If it hadn't been for Lipstick appealing to my gentler nature, he would've had more broken bones than Evel Knievel.'

Naomi's forehead furrowed. 'Where's Lipstick now?'

'In the spare bedroom.'

'In the…? Damn you, Karl.' Naomi stood angrily. 'Couldn't you have told me this before now?'

'Don't start all that again. Anyway, taking her back to her place wasn't an option, in case the scumbucket went looking for her. The doctor in the hospital administered a couple of heavy-duty painkillers. The last time I looked in, they were doing the trick. She was sleeping soundlessly.'

'I'll check on her,' Naomi said, walking quickly towards the landing.

'I'm going to get a wash and shave before we open up for business.' Karl waited a few seconds before easing his tired body off the sofa. He took a deep gulp of coffee, letting the dark oily liquid spark his battery. 'I just hope this day gets a lot better than this morning started.'

Little did he know, things where about to get a lot worse. A *hell* of a lot worse.

Chapter Five

You know, when you're little, you have more endurance than
God is ever to grant you again.
Children are man at his strongest. They abide.
Rachel Cooper, *The Night of the Hunter*

Scarman watched covertly from the house's back entry. Waiting with the patience of an apostle attending vespers. Cloaked appositely in the cowl of a monk, a nylon stocking pulled tightly over his face. He glanced at his luminous watch. Just gone four in the morning.

Those in the house had drunk their way through the evening with friends, screaming and cursing at each other like a bunch of wild apes, the jungle booze slithering down their monkey necks.

Earlier, cruising by in his van, feigning a lack of interest, he had witnessed an adult handing one of the children some sort of alcoholic beverage. The adult sniggered as the child made a disgusted face, before quickly puking out the liquid. A large dog quickly lapped up the vomit.

A fierce wind was blowing dustbins and their contents all about the small space where he stood. The dispersed bin lids rattled, clanking against walls and back doors, blending into a wintery cacophony. From an upturned bin, the carcass of a dead rat spilled out next to his boots. The rodent was shrouded in a shitty pair of knickers, shrivelled up like a piece of *papier mâché*. He kicked it down the alley, muttering something incoherent under his breath.

For the last thirty minutes or so, the vomit-eating dog Scarman had seen earlier in the day, was guarding the yard, snarling at him lurking in the darkness.

Fortunately for him, no-one seemed to care. A little while earlier, someone had drunkenly shouted from a window for the dog to shut the fuck up, but other than that, not a soul ventured outside into the freezing night air.

Despite the icy wind cutting to his marrow, he was certain the long wait would be worth it. Then, almost as if his thoughts contained magic, the last remaining lights were extinguished on the second floor, bringing total darkness inside and outside the house.

He waited a few minutes more. Then, from beneath his full-length overcoat, he removed a miniature crowbar, and began working it patiently around the weathered wood housing the galvanised backdoor bolt. Five minutes later, two twists of the wrists and a small amount of his unique brute force quietly splintered the designated area.

Easing the yard door open an inch, he watched the snarling beast looking up at him, its ears pinned back, exposed fangs now ready for action. The dog was some sort of half-breed mutt, ribs protruding cage-like from neglect and cruelty. There was madness in its eyes: a madness mirrored in his own.

'*Good dog…good dog…*' he whispered, removing a large piece of bloodied beef from a sealed bag in his pocket.

The dog continued snarling, but softer now, a low, suspicious growl, eyes flicking indecisively from food to intruder, before finally focusing on the food.

He slipped the beef halfway through the gap in the door, dangling it between his finger and thumb. The dog's nostrils widened, sniffing guardedly at the meat, before snapping it quickly from his fingers. In seconds, it was chewing hungrily on the rare manna from heaven.

Waiting until the creature was on the verge of swallowing the delicious substance, he struck like a cobra, entrapping the creature's throat in a vice-like clasp between powerful hands. Lifted effortlessly into the air in a fluid motion without thought, the dangling dog struggled, legs kicking out like a marionette with tangled strings.

He twisted the neck without fuss, hearing a watery snap, and then dropped the carcass where he stood, before moving towards the house.

From his pocket, he removed a skeleton key, grounded down to bypass the levels and wards inside the lock. The key had helped him a few times in the past, but nothing was guaranteed. He hoped he didn't have to use the crowbar.

That would slow down the building adrenalin rush of expectation trafficking his veins, and could also inadvertently alert those inside to his presence. He didn't mind killing, but he preferred it when everything was under control, moving at a tempo of his choosing.

He needn't have worried. The key's movement was silky-smooth, entering the dark passages of the chamber uninterrupted. He turned the key. It rotated fully. *Click*. The sound made his heart tighten slightly. He removed the key and turned the door handle ever so gently.

No resistance.

The door opened with just the tiniest of squeaks, and he invited himself inside, closing the door silently behind him. From a sheath on his belt, he removed a serrated hunting knife, gripping its carved ivory handle tightly. The knife's tiny teeth seemed to grin at him in the deadly dull darkness.

Pausing a few seconds to train his eyes to the house's structure, he proceeded inwards. From the living room, heavy snoring could be heard. He followed it, his great weight soundless. A man in a drunken stupor was sprawled out on a sofa, like a beached whale. The stench of stale booze, dead cigarettes and greasy soup filled the room. An ashtray struggled under a mound of cigarette butts resembling spent gun cartridges. The sleeping man farted loudly, rattling the sofa. He was sewer-stinking.

Pig…filthy drunken pig bastard…

Scarman's fingers gripped the knife's handle tighter. He wanted to use the blade. Gut this whale of a pig. Badly. Perhaps crack his skull. Work the crowbar into his brain, spoon out some meaty matter, shove it down the pig's throat.

No. Get in and out. He's not worth it. Keep focused. The prize is almost within reach. Yours for the taking.

He turned reluctantly, and began to make his way silently upstairs, thankful for the frayed carpet beneath his feet. Anticipation moved his heart up a notch. Even though he had never been in this house before tonight, his actions contained an unexplainable feeling of familiarity.

The first room he came to was a small bathroom, reeking of piss and a drunk's sour vomit. Someone hadn't flushed the toilet – possibly Mister Pig downstairs – and a large, cigar-coloured turd, the size of a baby's arm, floated helplessly, trying to escape its enclosure.

Dirty smelly pig…

He moved with purpose to the room at the end of the corridor, letting his emotions guide him, bring him home. The door was ajar. He stood outside. Listening. Heard breathing. Soft. Like a susurrus of insect wings in summer heat.

Inside the dull, moonlit room, the floor was scattered with dolls, mixed with little girl clothing. He knew that gold had been struck, and he the beneficiary.

My sweet lord…

He could hardly restrain his excitement at what he was

viewing. Two young girls in the bed, side-by-side, bedclothes scattered haphazardly. For a moment, he was overcome by the abundance, and had to steady his breathing and shaking hands. The feeling of iron in his penis made his teeth clench, his ballbag tighten. A plethora of unholy urges drilled deep into his body. He quickly erased them. For now.

Do what you came to do and get out. There'll be plenty of time for that, later.

Walking to the bed, he knelt down as if preparing nightly entreaties to a voyeuring deity. He could smell the girls' hot-body smells. Taste them. Exquisite. The richness touched the inside of his mouth, dusting his tongue with a taboo flavour. He almost wept with joy at this wealth of fleshy riches.

Take both? Impossible. One only. But which one?

They both seemed age-identical, but it was the one with red hair that his eyes kept returning to. Blood red, crowning an alabaster skin so beautifully white. A divine seraph from Heaven. Why did tormenting gods make them so beautiful; so teasingly beautiful? How was he, a mere mortal, supposed to resist such temptation?

Expertly shepherding the knife back into its enclosure, from his pocket he produced a silk handkerchief and a glass vial of chloroform. Dabbed the handkerchief with the colourless liquid, before gently tenting the girl's face in the damp silk. Applied pressure with his hand. Felt her hot, urgent breath mist the plummy flesh of his palm.

Her legs jerked violently, then quivered into serenity. The other child beside her had not moved, but mumbled in her sleep: stop kicking and taking all the bedclothes, Dorothy.

Dorothy…my beautiful Dorothy…

He quickly wrapped his prize in a blanket, before making his way back down the stairs. At the door, he set the limp little body down. Edging back into the living room, he stared down at the snoring pig on the sofa. His fingers touched the knife. He wanted desperately to gut him, ease the knife into the fleshy blubber. He wanted to hear Mister Pig grunt in agony.

But something made him hesitate. Just for a second. He stared at the full-to-the-brim ashtray. Smiled. The gods were good. They had given him the perfect cover-up.

Stepping outside a few minutes later, Scarman re-cradled Dorothy in his arms. Covered her in the custody of the cowl. Held her tightly, lest some thief in the night try to steal her from him. He moved across the yard as quickly and quietly as he had entered.

Just as he neared the busted yard door, a eucharistic moon bloomed forth from behind inky clouds. The moon's magnesium glow limned over him, tingling every bone in his taut body. He felt exposed, but in a sexual, all-powerful way. That was when he realised he was being watched.

He stopped. Corpse-still. Deadly-silent.

Where? Who?

Still cradling Dorothy, he slowly eased to the ground, kneeling, a demonic version of the *Pietà,* his eyes methodically scanning the darkness.

Something. What?

Then he saw the watcher. Eyes peering from behind a wall, a sentinel of the night. The face seemed to be grinning, mocking him in righteous judgement.

Placing Dorothy gently on the ground, he silently eased out the knife. Anticipation filled his nostrils and mouth. In the speed of an afterthought, he flung the knife into the darkness at the watching eyes.

Chapter Six

*It is not the violence that sets a man apart, it is the
distance that he is prepared to go.*
Forrest Bondurant, *Lawless*

Karl had just shifted himself from bed when the doorbell rang below. Four impatient rings.

'Shit, we've slept in, love,' Karl said, quickly slipping into
his trousers.

'Of course we slept in,' said Naomi. 'It's Saturday.'

'Saturday…? God, you're right. I thought it was Friday. My
head's away.'

Karl proceeded trance-like down the stairs, yawning constantly.

Four more impatient rings.

'All bloody right! I hear you!'

Opening the front door, he was greeted by a wide-awake
Sean, the postman, holding a small package.

'Morning, Karl.'

'Never mind that shite. Do you like sticking your bloody
fingers in holes that don't belong to you, Hans Brinker?'

'Who's Hans Brinker?'

'Read a book and find out.'

'I have to say, you look very rough, like you've been boozing and cruising when you should've been snoozing.'

'Another wannabe Seamus Heaney. Just what we don't need.'

'Just saying, I've seen you looking better.'

'Sorry I can't say the same about you.'

Sean smiled a wicket grin, handing Karl the package. 'At least it's not another rejected manuscript. Too small to be from–'

Karl slammed the door. Made his way upstairs, yawning some more. Once back inside, he sat on the sofa and began to open the package.

'What the...?' He took out the contents.

'What is it?' Naomi said, entering the room.

'An old beer mat, by the looks of it.' Karl held the piece of cardboard out to Naomi, while searching for a note from the sender. There was nothing.

'Who's it from?' Naomi examined the mat.

Karl shrugged his shoulders. 'Haven't a clue.'

'Fiddler's Green pub, that's what it says,' Naomi said.

Karl's face slapped awake. His stomach felt wobbly. He held out his hand. 'Let me see that again.'

Naomi handed it back. He scrutinised the front and then the back of the mat, staring at it as though it might speak.

'Karl? What's wrong?'

'Nothing...nothing's wrong...'

'There's *something* wrong. I can see it in your face. What on earth is it?'

'Nothing. I'm away to get cleaned up.' Karl stood and left the room, leaving a puzzled-looking Naomi staring at his back.

Inside the bathroom, he switched the power shower on full blast, before examining the beer mat more closely. He turned it over, back then front, hoping for a clue to its provenance. A creepy sensation like dry ice touched the stepping-stones of his spine. His haemorrhoids began throbbing, making him feel like shit.

Opening the medicine cabinet, he reached for a box of painkillers. Removed three from their enclosure. Put the box back. Washed the pills down with shower water. Walked over to the bathroom door and placed his back tight against it. From his trouser pocket he removed a small plastic bottle. Opened it, spilling two blue tablets into his palm. He dry-swallowed both, before sliding his back down the door.

He regarded the beer mat again, wondering. A feeling of dread began creeping over him. He needed to vomit, and vomit he did. Just as he wiped his mouth, the flashback hit him. Hard.

❊ ❊ ❊

A winter's night, outside Fiddler's Green, a popular restaurant and pub on the outskirts of Belfast, over twenty years ago.

Rain so heavy, it's practically deafening.

Karl is taking shelter behind a tree, one of many surrounding the restaurant. He's wearing a heavy-duty raincoat and wide-brimmed hat. The rain is sliding down the brim of the hat, splattering his face. Despite this, he has a good view of the restaurant, and in particular of a well-dressed man devouring a steak at a table near the window.

The man is a lover of food; his generous body-structure displays this proudly. If he had been a normal man, he would be overweight, but his size – length and breadth – has eliminated this, distributing fat and muscle evenly in almost perfect proportion.

From the inside pocket of his overcoat, Karl produces a gun – a Colt Cobra .38 Special revolver – a tiny gun with an immense impact. Opening up the gun's stomach, he checks the chambers again – the tenth time in as many minutes – unconsciously wiping the rain pellets from its metal skin. His hands are shaking, but not enough at the moment to retard what he has in mind: close up and personal.

The corner of Karl's eye catches movement. The man in the restaurant is standing, wiping juices from his mouth with a napkin. After some small-talk with a waitress, he hands her payment, smiles, then heads for the exit.

'*Shit!*' Karl shoves the gun into the overcoat's side pocket, grasping the weapon tightly in his hand.

The man is emerging from the doorway of Fiddler's Green,

fumbling with a black umbrella. The umbrella blossoms like a funereal flower, and the man is now walking in Karl's direction.

Karl slowly slides out the gun from his pocket, resting its compact weight against the side of his overcoat. He commences his walk towards the man. The rain is now torrential, beating against Karl's face, making clear vision impossible. It seems to be trying to hold him back.

The man moves slightly to the left, avoiding a puddle, as they pass. At the same time, Karl makes an identical move, and both men's arms touch, just slightly, but enough for Karl to release his grip on the gun.

To his horror, Karl watches the gun descend in slow motion, spinning and spinning. For one horrible second, he fears the irony of the gun going off, the bullet penetrating *his* head.

Both men stop in their tracks. The man looks at Karl. Karl can't move. Fear has immobilised him. The gun makes a noise as it hits the ground. Both men look down. Karl can see the gun, half-submerged in a filthy shallow puddle. Surely the man can see it also? The man stares at Karl.

'Sorry. This damn umbrella…I should've been looking where I was going.'

The man proceeds hurriedly onwards down the street. Karl stands in the sodden night, watching the distance consume the man; watching him become an inky exclamation mark, fading into a pixel. Then heavy nothingness.

Karl bends and pukes all over the ground, the gun, his shoes. The vomit mixes with the rain, becoming a Rorschach collage, two tiny accusing faces.

Move your arse. He's getting away!

Karl retrieves gun from puddle. Staggers after the man, swaying from side to side like a drunk. Pushes through the heavy nothingness. Sees the pixel. Watches it transform back into an exclamation mark. Then morphing into the man.

Karl's hands are shaking terribly, but he manages to pull back the hammer on the gun. Sees the back of the man's head. Squeezes down on trigger…

Chapter Seven

While money can't buy happiness, it certainly lets you choose your own form of misery.

Groucho Marks

Monday morning, and Karl had barely sat down for a quick liquid breakfast of coffee in the kitchen, when Naomi entered, smiling. She walked over and kissed his bare back.

'There's nothing as sexy as a man sitting in his underwear, drinking coffee, in the morning.'

A suspicious look appeared on Karl's face. 'What the hell are you on? Better still, what the hell are you up to?'

'Just telling the truth, big fella.'

Naomi placed the day's mail in front of him.

'That's bloody early. Bet that lazy bastard Sean has a birthday or something. That's why he's doing his rounds so quickly. So he can go out and get blitzed on cheap wine.'

'Oh, should we get him a card or something? He always makes sure we get our post, even when the weather's atrocious.'

'Wrong postal service. That's the Pony Express you're thinking of. Anyway, it's his job to get the mail here, isn't it? Do I get birthday cards for doing my job? Hell no. Abuse, that's what I get. Anything interesting in all that pile of crap?'

'Bills, love. All bills.'

'That's what I should have been called, instead of Karl. Bill. *Hmm*. Bill Kane. Has a ring to it, don't you think?'

'Not as sexy as Karl.'

'What's with the strange smile? You're up to something. What?'

'Nothing...' She ran her hand down his stomach, and into his underwear.

'If you're looking for my wallet, it's not there. But then again, I could be lying. If you keep looking, you just might get a surprise.'

'What kind of surprise?'

'That would be telling. You've got to keep searching. You might find two big rocks.'

'Show them to me later.' Naomi purred against his neck, and then removed her hand. From behind her back, she produced another letter. 'I think I forgot to give this to you.'

'For one scary moment, I thought you actually pulled that from under my ballbag.'

'It's from the bank.'

'From one ballbag to another. What do those bastards want now?'

'I don't know. I didn't read it.' A sly grin appeared on Naomi's face.

'*Hmm.* That's debateable,' Karl said, opening the letter and scanning its contents.

'Well?'

'Well what? You read it before me.' Karl gave Naomi a smile. 'The payment from the house has finally come through – as you already know. We're rich, my dear. Well, we would be, if most of it wasn't heading to Dad's nursing home for medical and care costs. But still, I think we–'

'Shoes. I need some shoes, badly.'

'You've more shoes than bloody Imelda Marcos.'

'And there's this little red dress I've been after.'

'Yes, I've been after one of those myself, for some time now.'

'And spending money…'

'Okay. You win. I'm not even going to argue with you. I suggest we close for the day, go on a little celebration.'

'Really?'

'No, make that a *large* celebration, starting right now.'

'Oh, Karl!'

Karl stood. They embraced. Kissing. Long, no-coming-up-for-air kissing, before collapsing on to the floor. Karl was thankful he was only wearing his underwear, but the gentle-man in him helped Naomi shed what little garments she was attired in at eight-thirty on a lovely, unusually sunny Monday morning in Belfast.

❄ ❄ ❄

For the longest time they rested there, on the soft, plush carpet, both sexually exhausted, listening to soft melodies whispering from the radio.

'I wish I had a house to sell every day, if that's the reward,' Karl said, grinning like a cat with milk *and* goldfish.

'You couldn't hack it, big lad. You've nothing left in the pipeline,' teased Naomi.

'Don't test me. I haven't even started using my reserves of oil, yet.'

The song on the radio came to an abrupt end. It was replaced by the local news, headlined by a house fire in north Belfast.

A family, named locally as the Reilly family, tragically perished in a blaze at their home in Victoria Barracks, in the early hours of yesterday morning. Neighbours reported hearing a loud explosion, before the house was engulfed in flames. Police believe a cigarette left burning by one of the occupants may have ignited a gas leak…

Chapter Eight

There are two of you, don't you see?
One that kills…and one that loves.
Roxanne, *Apocalypse Now*

Dorothy opened her eyes to a sea of claustrophobic gloom and semi-darkness pressing against her. Everything strange. Smells. Location. Time.

She tried moving, but arms and legs were swampy. As if bones had been separated from her body. An iron manacle ringed her left ankle. She pulled on the chain connected to it. No use. Fastened securely to the far wall. The effort sapped what little strength she had in her. Exhaustion took hold.

'Mum? Dad? Are you there?' she whispered fearfully, tears starting to glaze her eyes. *'Cindy…? Stop doing this to—'*

Without warning, a hand whipped around from behind, clamping her mouth tightly. She could barely breathe. Panicking, she lashed out, but was too weak to cause damage. Tears began flowing. Snot bubbled and spurted from her nose onto the gripping hand.

'Stop with the crying, and keep your voice down,' hissed a voice

into her ear. *'Scarman will hear you. If you force him to come, he'll punish us. If you make him come, I'll punish you, as well.'*

Dorothy stopped struggling as soon as she saw the owner of the hand. A girl, face filthy, ropey hair thick with grease. The girl cautiously removed her hand, before skidding the snot and tears back onto Dorothy's pyjamas.

'What's your name?' the girl asked.

'Dor…Dorothy. Dorothy Reilly.' Dorothy began wiping away the stream of tears and the leakage from her nose. She was finding it difficult not to sob. 'Where…where am I?'

'Not fucking Kansas, Dorothy – that's for sure.' The girl smiled, but not in a friendly way. 'We're in a big house, out in the shitty country somewhere. That's all I know.'

'What…am I doing here?'

'Are you serious? Can't you guess?'

'I…I'm not sure. I remember sleeping in bed with Cindy, my wee sister. There was a party…I don't know what happened after that.'

'Well, *I* can pretty much tell you what happened after that. You were taken.'

'What…?'

'Taken. Just like the movie. Scarman has you now.'

'Who…who's Scarman?'

'The Devil.'

Dorothy started puking. Most of the splattering slammed against the girl.

PAST DARKNESS

'You stupid little bitch! Look what the fuck you've done to my jeans!'

Dorothy began sobbing uncontrollably. She was in hell and the devil was coming for her.

Chapter Nine

It is not the oath that makes us believe the man,
but the man the oath.

Aeschylus

Naomi entered the office, giving Karl *the look*.

Shit. Not the look, thought Karl. *Please. Anything but that.*

It was Wednesday afternoon. Earlier in the morning, both Karl and Naomi had agreed to shorten the day, and hit the town for dinner and a couple of drinks. Well, possibly more than just a couple. The morning had been quite productive, and a nice advance for an upcoming job had been negotiated successfully.

'Don't give me that look, Naomi. I mean it. I'm not in the mood for it.'

'His name is Tommy Naughton. Looks desperate.'

'As desperate as me?' Karl said, putting on his desperate face.

'Worse.'

'Does Desperate Tommy look like he can pay handsomely for my services, with cold cash?'

Naomi shook her head. 'I would say probably not.'

'Can he at least pay uglier, via monthly instalments?'

'He doesn't appear to have a lot of money.'

'For god's sake, Naomi, this isn't a bloody charity! You should have hit him with an excuse.'

'I talked to Tommy for a couple of minutes. He's terribly upset.'

'*I'm* terribly upset, also, that you're already calling him by his first name. What did I warn you about falling for the Stockholm syndrome?'

'His daughter and her young family were killed in that terrible fire a couple of days ago, and they're being blamed for causing it themselves. Tommy doesn't believe it. He thinks no-one cares, because they came from a working-class area.'

'You know we're up to our necks in bills. I can't keep taking on charity cases, no matter how tragic. Otherwise we'll be the ones looking charity.'

Naomi stared at Karl, not saying a word.

'Don't do that with your eyes, Naomi. Stop it. It's not going to work, trying to make me feel bad.'

'You're not bad. You're good and decent. And kind. Otherwise I wouldn't be asking, and Tommy wouldn't be sitting out there hoping.'

'You do this every single bloody time to me, when I get a few quid ahead. I already told you, most of the money from the house has to go to Dad's health coverage.'

'Does that mean I can send Tommy in, my love?'

Karl sighed heavily. 'Okay, but here's the deal: He gets five minutes. Not a second more. After that, you come flying in on your broomstick and say I have an emergency, and need to leave immediately. Agreed?'

'I don't like lying. You know that.'

'And I don't like working for nothing. *You* know that. Anyway, that's the deal. Take it or leave it?'

Naomi waited a few seconds before answering. 'Okay…'

'That okay didn't sound too okay to me.'

'*Okay*,' Naomi said, turning her back on Karl and heading towards reception.

Tommy Naughton was ushered in the door. In his fifties and of slight build, he was dressed in a withered shirt and tie, and a dark-grey suit that had seen better days. His shoes, however, were gleaming like a tongue of oil in sunlight.

Karl immediately thought of the old Cherry Blossom legend his father always quoted to him as a kid: *A shine on your shoe says a lot about you.*

'Mister Kane?'

'That's me. And you are Mister Naughton.' Karl offered a handshake.

Tommy nodded, and shook Karl's hand. The shake was firm. Karl could feel the toughened calluses of a lifelong bricklayer or steel erector: a struggler in life's perpetual grinding of soul and body.

'Grab yourself a seat, Mister Naughton.'

'Thank you for seeing me, Mister Kane,' Tommy said, sitting down. 'I know how busy you are, but I'm at my wits' end. My daughter Pauline, son-in-law Charlie Reilly and two granddaughters, Dorothy and Cindy, died in a house fire, last week gone. Now their names are being dragged through the mud into the bargain.'

'My condolences, Mister Naughton. A horrible tragedy. I heard some parts on the news. From what I gathered, there was a large explosion?'

Tommy looked uncomfortable. 'The entire house practically disintegrated. They couldn't even find all the bodies, it was that devastating. Charlie…did a bit of wheeling-and-dealing, selling propane bottled gas at a knockdown price from his back yard. The place was packed with them.'

'I see…'

'I…I'm not trying to justify it. It was a catastrophe waiting to happen, and I told him that hundreds of times, but he did whatever he could to feed his family. Selling black-market gas made a few extra quid to keep his family afloat.'

And probably ended up killing them, Karl wanted to say, but didn't.

'What exactly is it you're hoping I can do?'

'The peelers are trying to make it out that Charlie or Pauline fell asleep smoking, while gas was leaking in the house. They're blaming them for everything.'

'You think differently, of course?'

'They never smoked in their lives.'

'Oh…I see.' Karl pondered for a moment before continuing. 'Didn't I read something about a party going on, well into the night? Could it have been one of the guests smoking, someone drunk, messing about? You know yourself how a party can get out of hand, once people start drinking.'

'The party was a little get-together to celebrate Pauline's thirty-fifth birthday. I know some of the ones at the party, and they're smokers and a bit wild, but they'd all gone home, hours before the fire. There was no-one in the house except Pauline, Charlie and the kids, at the time of the explosion.'

'So why do the police say they suspect one of the parents had been smoking?'

'You'd have to ask them that,' Tommy responded, his voice tightening with anger.

'Without meaning to sound flippant, couldn't you have asked them?'

'I live in the New Lodge, Mister Kane. In case you're not familiar, the New Lodge is a tough nationalist area. People there don't talk to the peelers without ending up with a six-pack.'

Karl looked confused. 'A six-pack?'

'Shot in both knees, elbows and ankles.'

Karl made a pained face. 'That's rough punishment for just talking to cops.'

'Anyway, why would the peelers listen to someone like me

contradicting them? Now, someone like *you*, with a reputation? That's different. I've read all about you.'

'You have?' Karl's face brightened.

'You don't take crap from anyone.'

Karl looked in the direction of Naomi, sitting behind her desk in the reception. 'That's debatable.'

From his suit's inside pocket, Tommy removed a brown envelope. 'I know you're the best and don't come cheap. There's three hundred quid in there. That's a lot of money to me, Mister Kane, but it'll be well spent if you take the case on.'

'Three hundred...?' Karl almost smiled. 'In all honesty, three hundred wouldn't get me very far. Barely cover my expenses for a day.'

'I can get more, if you're willing to give me some time to get it. I know a couple of loan sharks who'll help me.'

'Sharks don't help, they devour.' Karl shook his head. 'It's not just the money. In all honesty, I wouldn't have the time needed to dedicate myself to such a serious and complex matter. What I can do is give you the number of a good solicitor I know. She'll be able to–'

Just then, Naomi rushed through the door, startling both Karl and Tommy. 'Tell Karl where the money came from, Tommy.'

'What? Oh. Well...I've been saving up for a holiday, me and Theresa – that's my wife. She's been very sickly. We haven't had a good holiday in ages, so I've been saving to take her somewhere nice. Derrybeg in Donegal, hopefully.'

'Derrybeg?' Karl said, voice filling with suspicion. 'What a strange coincidence, eh, Naomi?'

'And no better place,' said Derrybeg woman, Naomi, smiling proudly. 'The greatest wee town in the greatest county in Ireland, Donegal.'

Karl glared at Naomi. Closed his angry eyes. When he reopened them, they were filled with resigned defeat.

'Okay, here's the score, Mister Naughton. I'll look into what you've told me, but I can't promise anything more than that. Understood?'

For the first time since entering the premises, Tommy Naughton smiled with relief, as if a ton weight had been lifted from his shoulders. He stood. Put out his hand.

'That's good enough for me, Mister Kane.'

Karl shook the hand. 'Just remember: no promises.'

'Thank you, Mister Kane. Thank you.'

'Leave your contact details with Naomi. I'll get back to you as soon as possible.'

Tommy turned to leave.

'Take this with you,' Karl said, holding out the envelope. 'We can come to some sort of financial arrangement later. Take your wife on that holiday.'

Tommy looked at the envelope, then at Karl. 'Thank you, Mister Kane.'

'There's one more thing I need you to do for me, Tommy.'

'You just name it, Mister Kane, and it's done.'

'Can you stop calling me Mister Kane? It makes me feel… old. Karl will suffice. And for good measures, I'll stop calling you Mister Naughton. Agreed, Tommy?'

'You've got it, Karl,' Tommy said, leaving the room escorted by a smiling Naomi.

Karl waited until Naomi returned.

'What happened to our deal? Weren't you meant to rush in on your broomstick and say I had an emergency?'

'But I did rush in, and it *was* an emergency.' Naomi smiled wickedly. Leaned over the desk, and kissed the love of her life hard on the mouth.

'You know this is going to end up costing me money? It always does.'

'Do you want to take my panties down and spank me for being naughty and disobeying you?'

'I can hardly take *my* panties down, I'm so weak with hunger at the moment. We'll keep that for tonight, when I've more energy to *debrief* you. Now, let's get the hell out of here, before someone else shows up thinking this is a charity shop. I'm so hungry, I'd eat the back door buttered. Oh, just one other thing.'

'Yes, my dearest?'

'Antrim is the greatest county in Ireland.'

Chapter Ten

Murderers are not monsters, they're men. And that's the most frightening thing about them.
Alice Sebold, *The Lovely Bones*

'Have you finished throwing up all over me?' the girl said, watching Dorothy removing vomit from her mouth with the sleeve of her pyjamas.

Dorothy spat out the remaining lumps of sourness in her mouth, before nodding. 'I…I'm sorry…didn't mean to vomit on you.'

'You're lucky I didn't give you a good punch in the gob. I had to go change from my last rags into these even shittier ones.'

'I'm really sorry–'

'Enough of that "sorry" shit. I heard you the first time. There's a box of old clothes in there, all ripped but they'll help keep you warm. They belonged to some old woman. Look at this stupid old sweater I'm wearing, with these stupid teapot designs on it.'

Dorothy stripped off her vomit-stained pyjama top, and found a sweater to pull over her head. It was much too big, and the wool was scratchy and uncomfortable. A terrible stench of damp and mould seemed to be imbedded in the material.

'Thank...thank you.'

'Don't thank me. Thank the dead old bag who owned it. Sometimes at night in the dark, I think I can smell her in here.'

Dorothy stood very still. Shadows were moving in the darkness. She wanted to scream.

'One night, it was so cold in here,' continued the girl, 'I had to stick on a pair of her knickers to try and keep warm. After a minute of being inside them, I felt something scratching my hole.'

'Don't! Please...don't talk like that. It scares me.'

'Scares you? How d'you think I felt, when I found a whole family of spiders living in her drawers?'

Dorothy started scratching, as if the spider family had moved from one garment to the next. She was certain there was something moving about in the sweater.

'Can I sit down, please, on your mattress?'

'Park your arse, if you want.'

Dorothy sat on the edge of the mattress.

'Can...can I ask your name?'

The girl thought for a minute before answering. 'People call me all sorts of names. Bitch, scum, whore....'

Dorothy's face flushed. She quickly looked away.

'What's wrong?' The girl was smiling her scary, leery grin.

'Trying to tell me you never heard those words before? What are you, a wee goody-goody girl?'

'No….'

'Okay, Miss Good-Goody, you can call me Tara.'

Dorothy looked about the bare room, trying to think of something that wouldn't incur this strange and frightening girl's wrath or ridicule.

'How…how long've you been here, Tara?'

'Long? Very…very long. It stays dark most of the time, because the windows are boarded up, so it's hard to tell night or day. Scarman took me when I was buying cigs in the wee shop at the corner of–'

'You smoke?'

'Don't you?'

'No.'

'You really are a wee goody-goody. I'm gasping for a cig, right now.'

'My mum and dad would kill me if they thought I smoked.'

'I don't have a ma or da, so I don't give a shit. I do as I please. Always have.'

'You don't have a mum or a dad?' Dorothy was shocked.

'Have you socks in your ears or something? I hate repeating myself.'

'I've never met anyone without a mum or dad. It must be terrible.'

'Why?'

Dorothy shrugged her shoulders. 'I don't know. Just seems so sad. I would hate not to have my mum and dad.'

'From what I was told, my ma and da weren't up to much anyway. Give me away when I was three months old, the bastards. Anyway, enough sob stories. Do you want to hear about Scarman, or not?'

Dorothy reluctantly nodded. In truth, monsters were the last things she wanted to hear about in this house of horror.

'When I came out of the wee shop, Scarman was standing beside a van. He had a photo of a wee girl. He tried showing me it, saying it was his daughter, she was lost, and had I seen her.'

'What did you do?'

'I'm nobody's fool. I ignored the bastard. He made a grab for me, but I kicked him in the balls, hard.'

'You *kicked* him? Are you joking?'

'He's not the first scumbag I've kicked in the balls. It was sweet, watching his ugly, scarred face fill with pain.'

'Then what happened?'

'I clawed his revolting gob. Took his skin clean off. Broke a couple of fingernails, but it was worth it. I don't remember much more than that. I think he poured something over my face to knock me out, some sort of drug, probably.'

Dorothy's voice suddenly filled with despair. 'He's gonna do dirty things to us and kill us, isn't he, just like on TV?'

She started sobbing, her shoulders shaking violently like a

pneumatic drill. Tara's hand reached out to Dorothy's shoulder, but stopped before touching it, as if fearful of contamination.

'Listen to me, and listen good. You do anything you need to do to survive in here. *Anything*. Got that?'

Dorothy didn't answer. She continued sobbing, quieter now.

'Don't you want to see your ma and da again, and your wee sister?'

Dorothy sniffed. 'Yes…'

'You will, but not if you keep crying. Sometimes you have to die to stay alive.'

'But…I don't want to die.'

'I mean die inside. Do things that are horrible.'

'I don't want to do horrible things.'

'Then you will die. *Really* die, and Scarman will win. Do you want him to win?'

'No…'

Tara brought her face right up against Dorothy's. 'Then remember this: you do anything you need to do to survive. *Anything*. Right?'

Dorothy was hit by the stench of Tara's bad breath, and lack of washing. It was overwhelming, but despite wanting to puke, she knew better than to let it show on her face.

'O…kay…I…I'll try…'

'You better do more than try.'

Dorothy started sniffing the air, screwing her face up. 'What's that terrible smell? It's disgusting, like rotten cabbage.'

Tara pointed nonchalantly towards the far corner, where a rusted metal bucket lurked.

'You have to use it if you need to take a shit or a pee. The chain on your leg stretches to the far corner, so you can get to it easily enough. Sometimes, Scarman brings old newspapers to wipe your arse with. It's rough, but better than nothing.'

Dorothy pinched her nose. 'I…I couldn't use that thing. It's horrible.'

'Then you'll shit yourself, won't you? Do, and you'll not be on this mattress for long. I can tell you that for nothing.'

'But…you'll be watching me go to the toilet.'

'Why would I want to watch you taking a shit? Think I'm sick?'

'No, of course not. I….'

'Just be careful Scarman isn't watching, though. He has a wee peep-hole in the door.' Tara grinned.

'Don't say that. I'll just hold it in.'

'Then you'll burst open, won't you? That should be fun.'

'That's not funny…'

'Look, if it helps, just pretend you're out camping in the woods, and this room is your tent. That's what I do. Scarman comes every other day and cleans the pot out. He also brings scraps of food with him when–'

'Oh, my stomach. I'm gonna be sick.' Dorothy began to retch violently.

'Not on this mattress, you're not!' Tara kicked Dorothy roughly off the mattress with her foot. 'Use the bucket if you want to puke.'

Dorothy went rush-crawling to the bucket, as if her very life depended upon it. She retched like hell, before puking her stomach out. After a few minutes, she returned to the mattress, shaking terribly, tears rolling down her face.

'I...I feel horrible...'

'Get used to it.'

'Can't...can't you stop tormenting me, just for a second?'

Tara forced a laugh. Stared directly into Dorothy's face.

'You should be thanking me. You said you couldn't use the bucket, but you did. Lesson learned. There'll be other things you don't want to do in here, terrible things, but you better learn to do them if you want to survive.'

'You...you're a...horrible person.'

'I'm not here to babysit a baby. I'm here to survive. With or without you, I intend to escape, and I won't let you get in the way with all your moaning.'

'Escape?' Dorothy's face lit up. 'Will...will you take me with you, Tara? Please. I'll do anything you ask, if only–'

'So, you *will* do anything, after all, when it suits? See how easy it can be, once you set your mind to it?'

'You...you *will* take me with you, won't you?'

PAST DARKNESS

Tara began to smile, like a fox with a chicken clamped firmly in its jaws. 'Of course. I would never dream of leaving you behind…'

Chapter Eleven

Doubt everything. Find your own light.
Gautama Buddha

Next morning, despite a buzz-saw hangover, Karl phoned his best friend, forensic pathologist Tom Hicks.

'Tom? How're things?' Karl stationed his mobile between shoulder and ear, attempting to read the obituary page in the morning newspaper, killing the myth that men can't multi-task, at least some of the time.

Hicks' voice sounded tired and raw. 'Apart from dying with flu, migraines and backache, I'm still breathing. I haven't been able to get out of bed in days. I can't even–'

'Okay, enough about you. Time is money. I need a bit of info, on the fire last week in the New Lodge, where the entire family died.'

'The Reilly family? What about it?'

'I've a client seriously doubting the official version. He's the father of one of the victims. Was there anything strange, anything out of the ordinary, about the case?'

Karl could hear Hicks move slightly, as if trying to get comfortable in the bed.

'Apart from some irresponsible person stacking over fifty bottles of propane gas beside a wall and causing an explosion?'

'Apart from that, yes.'

'I haven't read the full report. Barney Blaney is standing in for me. But from what I *did* read and was able to discern, the fire started in the kitchen, or in the proximity to it, and was probably caused by a cigarette that wasn't fully extinguished.'

'Could the fire have been started maliciously?'

'All things are possible, but let me give you a few statistics before you start making assumptions and getting yourself into trouble. Kitchens are *the* principal area of origin for home fires, and smoking is a leading cause of fire deaths. Eighty percent of all fire-deaths occur when people are asleep. Put alcohol into the mix, and you've an invite for disaster. Those are the hard facts, and appear to be cohesive in this scenario, as well as backing up Blaney's report.'

Karl thought for a moment. 'Do you rate Blaney's judgement?'

There was a slight pause. 'Well…he's a highly qualified and competent pathologist. He knows his stuff. Foul play was ruled out, more or less.'

'More or less?' Karl added a suspicious tone to his voice.

'Nothing has been conclusively established, because of the sheer ferocity of the fire caused by the explosion. The house practically disintegrated, along with the adjacent building, a grocery shop. Not all the bodies were accounted for, or what was left of them.'

'Why do you think that was?'

'Instantaneously vaporised, is one appalling explanation. Or pure incineration. Coupled with this were the gale-force winds that morning, and throughout the day, creating extreme conditions that would have hindered finding all particles from the bodies.'

'I see…'

'When you say it like that, you clearly don't see at all. Look, if it makes your client feel better, ninety-nine percent of the time, friends and family are wracked with guilt at not having been able to prevent the unpreventable. They end up conjuring conspiracy theories about fires being started deliberately. Ninety-nine percent of the time they are wrong, of course.'

'What about the other one percent, who *are* proven right?'

There was a five-second stony silence before Hicks replied.

'That's why they hire people like *you*, Karl, hoping to prove people like *me* wrong.'

Chapter Twelve

If you want to keep a secret, you must also hide it from yourself.
George Orwell, *1984*

'**D**o you want to see something?' Tara said, grinning at Dorothy.

'What?'

'A secret.'

'What kind of secret?'

'The best kind. The dangerous kind.'

Dorothy didn't want to be part of any secrets this strange girl might have, especially dangerous secrets, but she also didn't want to insult her.

'What is it?'

Tara turned, edged up to the top of the old horsehair mattress. Slid her hands inside. When she extracted her hands, she was holding three items: an ancient cutthroat razor; a busted cigarette lighter; and a miniature, moth-eaten teddy bear, encrusted in dirt, most of its face missing.

'I've been chipping beneath the boarded-up window with this old razor. I've already made a wee spy-hole to see outside. If we make it bigger, we can escape. The wood isn't very strong. It's filled with woodworm. This whole shitty place is falling down.'

'Won't that take forever, using that rusty razor?'

'Not now that there's two of us. Don't you see? I can work away at the wood, while you listen out for Scarman.'

The mere mention of Scarman's name made Dorothy's stomach percolate with nerves. 'But…what if he finds out? Won't…won't he punish us?'

'The trick is not to let him find out, isn't it? Any wee bits of wood from the cutting, I shove it out through the hole. That's what I've been doing, every chance I get.'

'But how are you able to reach the window from here? It's so far away.'

'Not when you can do this.' Tara arched herself downwards towards her ankles, her hands pulling slowly on the manacle. Within seconds, she had slipped her bare foot out of the metal enclosure.

Dorothy looked on in amazement.

'How…how did you do that?'

'I'm double-jointed. It comes in handy when I break into houses to steal. Give it a try. You might be double-jointed as well, without even knowing it. Go on. Try it.'

'Okay…' Dorothy took a deep breath before reluctantly carbon-copying each of Tara's moves. She slowly pulled on her ankle. Her face cringed. 'That's sore! My skin's coming off!'

'Can't you stop fucking moaning for a second? It's only a scratch. Try it again.'

Gritting her teeth, Dorothy reluctantly attempted the manoeuvre again. This time, blood appeared beneath the shredded skin. 'Arhhhhhhhh! I'm bleeding!'

'It's nothing. A wee speck.'

'It's not a wee speck. And it's sore.'

'It'll toughen you up. You'll need that, if you want to get out of here, and beat this bastard. You need to keep trying it, every chance you get, wee bit by wee bit. Eventually, you'll be able to get your foot free from the chain.'

'I…I'm sure there are people looking for me, right now. My mum and dad won't give up until they find me. They'll rescue me.'

'Stop fooling yourself. No one's gonna rescue you, except you. Get that through your thick head.'

'Why are you being so nasty to me? I didn't do anything to you, did I?'

'Shut the fuck up!'

'Okay…I…I don't want to make you angry. I'll keep quiet, if that's what you want.'

'Just stop getting on my nerves and messing up my head! I was fine until you came here, asking question after question.'

Watching Tara pace up and down, mumbling, tightened Dorothy's stomach like a taut spring. There was something unpredictable, malevolent even, about Tara that frightened the life out of her.

After a few minutes of pacing, Tara said, 'I saw an old man

walking along the grass-way, the other night. I think he was a farmer, the way he was dressed, and walking like a duck. I flicked the lighter a few times, you know, like Morse code, hoping he'd see me.'

'What's Morris code?'

'Morse, not Morris. Don't you know anything? I can't be arsed explaining everything to you. Morse code is like secret signals.'

'How would the farmer know if it's secret?'

'You really are daft, aren't you? C'mere. Let me show you something.'

Tara walked to the door. Dorothy hobbled behind her.

'Do you see that metal box inside the door?' Tara said, pointing.

'Where the keyhole is?'

'Behind that is a large bolt. That's what Scarman locks the door with. Not a key.' Tara placed her shoulder against the wall, and began snaking her arm through the tiniest of gaps in the plaster. A moment later, Dorothy could hear metal scraping against metal.

She watched in horror and amazement as the door creaked, opening a sliver.

Tara smiled at the look on Dorothy's face.

'I don't blame you for looking scared. Sometimes even I get the shits, putting my arm out there, as if he's waiting with a big butcher's knife, ready to slice my arm off.'

'Won't…won't he…see it open?'

'No, I can slide it back in place without him knowing. A couple of times, when I heard his van drive away, I sneaked down the stairs, looking for grub.'

'You didn't, did you? You're mad for doing that.'

'Mad…?' Tara seemed hypnotised by the word. 'Yes I am, aren't I? That's what they said about me in Blackmore.'

'Aren't you terrified, putting your arm out?'

'Shitting bricks, but I get a real strange thrill in my stomach, as if it's being tickled from inside. It's like, don't do it, but the more I tell myself not to, another part of me is daring myself to do it. Like a devil and an angel, on my shoulders.'

'What's downstairs?'

'Rooms. Lots of rooms. All the windows are boarded, with wood and metal bars across them. The front and back doors can only be opened from outside. I tried getting out, but it's no use. I found some hard bread, though, in a filthy cupboard in the kitchen. Rats had been feeding on it, but it was delicious.'

Dorothy made a puke face. 'You ate filthy bread touched by rats?'

'You think you wouldn't? Just wait until you get pains in your stomach from the hunger. You'll wish you had a slice, even a crust, anything to stop the pain and cramps.'

'I don't care how hungry I was, I'd never eat it.'

'You said that about the bucket…' Tara put her arm back out through the gap, securing the bolt in its rightful place.

A wobbly smile of relief appeared on Dorothy's face, seeing the closed door.

'Why do I feel safer now that it's closed, Tara?'

'Fear. You're filled with it. You've got to overcome it, face it. That's how I survived in Blackmore.'

'Blackmore? You keep saying that. What is it?'

'The orphanage I was in, until I escaped. They used to scare the girls in there, with talk of the devil taking them away if they didn't do what they were told. There was an old tower in the centre of the yard. It was black with age, like something out of a horror story. Pastor Kilkee always told us, that's where Satan comes at night, watching. If we didn't do things for him, Satan would take us away with him, to Hell.'

Dorothy shuddered involuntarily. 'Don't talk about...you know, "S". I don't like hearing his name.'

'Satan? Ha! Know what I did when they told me Satan was in that big dark tower?'

'I don't want to know.'

'One night, I sneaked right over there in the pitch dark, a black candle and a deck of cards in my hands. I lit the candle, and spread all the cards out in front of me. It started raining, thunder and lightning, the entire fucking show. Then I called Satan up from–'

Dorothy placed her hands tight against her ears, trying to block the sound of Tara's words from her head, hobbling back to the mattress.

'Please, Tara, stop talking about–'

'–Hell, told him to take me away.'

'Stop it!'

'Next thing I knew, footsteps started coming up the stairs. Really weird footsteps, like a goat would make. The footsteps were getting closer and closer. Then I saw him – yellow eyes, fangs, tail, face all hairy…'

'*Stopppppppppp it!*'

'It was Bonzo.'

Dorothy slowly took her hands away from her ears. 'What…?'

'Bonzo. The cook's shaggy dog.'

'Dog…?'

'That's right. Not Satan, but a stupid dog. Next thing I know, Bonzo's licking my face and wagging his tail, like I'm this big dog biscuit. That was when I knew, there's no such thing as Satan. That was when I knew, I had the power to overcome my fear. That was when the staff began to fear *me*, especially Pastor Kilkee…'

Chapter Thirteen

As a dog returns to its own vomit…
Proverbs 26:11

Karl's car rolled to a slow halt outside the Naughton home. He looked out the side window, disbelieving the scene before his eyes.

'What the hell…?'

The street resembled a war zone. A large gap conspicuously glared at him from across the street, where the house and the grocery shop had recently been. Windows in other houses were boarded up with wooden shields.

As Karl emerged from the car, Tommy Naughton came out of the house, greeting him with an outstretched hand.

'Thank you for coming, Karl.'

'Not a problem, Tommy.'

'My goodness, that's some car you're driving,' Tommy said, staring at Karl's most cherished possession. 'Is that a Ford Cortina GT?'

'You have the eye, Tommy.'

'They don't make them like that any more. A classic.'

'You'll never believe where I got it,' Karl said, beaming with pride.

'Where?'

'Remember *The Sweeney* TV show?'

'Are you kidding?' Tommy's eyes lit up. 'One of my favourite shows, from the seventies. Regan and Carter, John Thaw and Dennis Waterman?'

'Well, that beauty of mine was one of the original ones used on the show. I bought it from a man who worked in the BBC. They were actually going to scrap it. Can you believe that?'

Tommy shook his head. 'Sacrilege.'

'Exactly. Cost me a fortune. I've had it restored, bit by bit, over the years.'

'I can see that, and what a job you've done on it. A beauty, as you say.'

Karl was quickly warming to Tommy. Few people – notably unappreciative Naomi – truly understood the appeal of the car, or the dedication needed to maintain its beauty and longevity.

'I could talk all day about the car, Tommy, but unfortunately I have to change the subject.' Karl cast his eyes across the street. Kids were chasing each other across the stark gap in the streetscape. 'When you told me about the fire, I didn't realise just how devastating it'd been.'

'I know. Shocking to look at. And what remained of the two buildings has already been pulled down, for safety reasons.'

'I can see the kids are taking no heed of that.'

'It isn't for the kids' safety. It's for the safety of the peelers. The kids have been throwing bricks at them, so they've had the remains demolished and all the bricks removed. The Housing Executive is refusing to replace the broken windows in the other houses – ours included. They only replace broken windows caused by rioting, not by gas explosions.'

'Are you serious?'

'You know, people in this area don't have a lot of money. Replacing widows is expensive.'

Karl shook his head in disbelief. 'Only in Belfast would they encourage a riot to have broken windows replaced.'

'Come inside. I'll get Theresa to make some tea.'

As he was about to enter Tommy's home, Karl hesitantly asked, 'I don't mean to offend you, Tommy, or the good people living here, but…well, do you think my car'll be safe? I'd hate to see anything happen to it.'

Tommy smiled. Winked. 'Don't worry about that. No-one in this area will mess with your car when they see whose house it's parked outside. Guaranteed.'

Inside the small, terraced residence, Karl was ushered into the parlour by Tommy.

'I'll be back in a sec, Karl. Got to get the boss.'

The parlour was spotlessly clean, filled with knick-knacks, alongside religious pictures adorning the walls. Small, framed photos of Pope John Paul II and John F Kennedy sandwiched a larger one of the Sacred Heart. Across the room, resting atop a fireplace, a group of family photos was displayed. A china cabinet in the corner was packed with Capodimonte porcelain figures, and for a brief, melancholy moment, Karl thought of his father giving such figures to his mother, home from trips around the world as a merchant seaman.

True to his word, a few seconds later, Tommy returned along with a small woman with piercing eyes.

'Karl? This is Theresa, the wife and boss.'

Theresa Naughton's hair was proudly grey, with no cover-up dye. Despite the passage of time, her striking good looks were still prominent in the bone structure of her face, all captained by that pair of commanding eyes.

'Mister Kane. I've heard so much about you. Thank you for coming.' Theresa extended her hand. Karl shook it, gently.

'Not a problem, Theresa, and please, just call me Karl.'

'Karl it is. Let me get you a nice cup of tea.'

'If I'm not being too cheeky, Theresa, would you have any coffee?'

'I love a cheeky man, Karl. Coffee you shall have. Sit yourself down, take the weight off your feet.'

Tommy waited until Theresa had left the room. 'She's taken a shine to you. It's not everyone she makes coffee for.'

'I seem to have that hypnotic power over all beautiful women, Tommy. I just can't help myself. I'm a wee bit puzzled, though.'

'Puzzled?'

'For such a sickly woman, she looks very healthy, if you don't mind me saying?'

'I'll go give her a hand,' Tommy said, quickly leaving the room.

Outside in the street, a Mister Whippy ice-cream van had pulled up. Its Pied Piper jingle almost instantly conjured up zombie-like children out of nowhere, drawn magnetically towards it.

'Freezing out there, and they still want ice cream,' Theresa said, entering the room a few minutes later, followed by Tommy carrying a tray laden with goodies: coffee in a Shelley fine-bone coffee pot; sugar and milk occupying small silver containers; an army of assorted biscuits overflowing the plate.

'She only gets this out if the Pope's coming to visit,' Tommy grinned.

'Behave yourself, Tommy Naughton,' Theresa said, smiling. 'Don't be shy, Karl. Get tucked in. A big man like yourself needs his grub.'

Karl poured himself a coffee, and took a biscuit out of politeness. He sipped the hot liquid.

'This is a great cup of coffee, Theresa. Haven't tasted one like it in ages.'

Theresa smiled, and Karl swore she was blushing. Theresa reached over and removed one of the photos on the fireplace. She began pointing out the people in the picture.

'This is our daughter Pauline, and son-in-law Charlie. And those two wee angels are Dorothy and Cindy. All gone to their reward now.'

Karl took the photo and nodded. 'A beautiful family, Theresa.'

'Do you have any grandchildren, Karl?'

'Not for another few years, I hope.' Karl laughed nervously. 'I've one daughter. Katie.'

'Katie. That's a beautiful Irish name. Katherine, meaning pure and clear.'

'Well, she certainly has made me financially *poor* over the years, that much is very *clear*.' Karl handed the framed photo back, his cynical nature suspecting Theresa of wanting him to see the family as real people – people he would begin to care about, rather than just names in the newspapers.

'Do you genuinely think you'll be able to clear Pauline and Charlie's names, Karl? Tommy seems to think so.'

Karl looked at Tommy, then back at Theresa.

'What I told Tommy was – and I was quite clear on this – I would look into it, but *couldn't* promise any results. There's not a lot I can do unless someone tells me something they didn't tell the police. From what Tommy tells me, no one around here would tell the police anything. But they'll probably regard an outsider like me as some sort of cop as well, and give me the cold shoulder, if not a hot fist in the mouth.'

'We have a saying around here: It's often a person's mouth that breaks his nose. But word has been sent out that you're okay, Karl.' Theresa's voice spoke with authority. 'You'll be getting no punches. If anyone knows anything, word will come back to me and I'll see you get it.'

'That helps, but I have to be honest. I spoke to a good friend of mine in-the-know, a highly respected pathologist. He's looked at the report, and according to him, everything seems above-board. He reckons the cops have it right.'

Just then, in walked a beautiful mackerel tabby cat, the distinctive 'M' stamped across its forehead. The cat had attitude and was having a bad fur day. It looked maniacal, like it had just escaped from a cat asylum, or had forgotten to take its medication.

It stared up at Karl, its green eyes narrowing like Clint Eastwood confronting an adversary in a spaghetti movie. Around its neck, a tiny bauble dangled.

'That's Tiddles. You're sitting on her seat,' Theresa said, smiling. 'She'll try to intimidate you by dead-eyeing you, but just ignore her. Whatever you do, don't stroke her. She hates being stroked by men.'

'That's something Tiddles and I have in common then. I don't like to be stroked by men either.' Karl returned the smile, even though the damned cat was making him nervous with its hypnotic stare. 'To be honest with you, I'm not the greatest of cat-lovers.'

Theresa shrugged her shoulders. 'That's okay, not everyone is. Cats aren't like dogs. They do as they see fit. Bet you're a dog lover?'

'No, it's got nothing to do with that. A few years ago, my ex-wife threw her…' Karl almost said 'pussy', but quickly corrected himself. '…cat in my face.'

'My goodness!' Theresa looked horrified. 'What a horrible thing to do. Poor thing.'

Karl knew for certain that Theresa's words of sympathy were directed squarely towards the cat.

'I still have a few scars its claws gave me, above my left eye.' Karl shifted his head slightly, where dull sunlight was coming in through the window, but Theresa didn't seem interested in his wounds.

'Did the RSPCA get their hands on the dreadful woman?'

'No.'

'Scandalous. Surely to God they could've charged her with something?'

Having an affair with another woman, whose dick was bigger than mine?

'Unfortunately, no, Theresa.'

After a few more minutes of small talk, Karl finished his coffee and stood to leave. 'I'll start checking out some of your neighbours tomorrow, see if they can add anything to what you've already told me. Other than that, you have my card. Call me if you can think of anything.'

'Thank you for coming, Karl. It really is appreciated,' Theresa said, standing.

'I hope you enjoy your holiday, down in Donegal,' Karl said.

Theresa looked puzzled. 'Holiday? What holiday?'

'Oh, I'm sorry. I've let the cat out of the bag, so to speak. Didn't Tommy tell you about the holiday he has planned for you?' Karl smiled wickedly at an uncomfortable-looking Tommy.

'Huh! It'll be a first, him taking me anywhere.'

'Well, a little bird named Naomi told me that's all about to change.' Karl turned his attention on Tommy. 'Isn't that right, Tommy?'

Tommy's face was performing nervous ticks. 'What? Oh, yes. Of course…of course…it was my little surprise, darlin'.'

'More a shock than surprise,' Theresa said, eyeing Tommy suspiciously.

Outside, rain was coming down in thick, dirty grey pellets. Karl gave the car a good once-over, dreading the prospect of nail-lines or dents. Nothing. He smiled with relief. Quickly got in. He adjusted the mirror, momentarily framing a man, seemingly staring at him from across the street. Tall. Stocky. Defiant.

Karl started the engine, and then spun the car around, slowly passing the man. He was dressed in a dark, heavy rain-coat, buttoned to the throat. A hat hung low, its brim covering most of the forehead and the hedges of eyebrows. Something black loitered in his right hand, and for one heart-stopping moment, Karl thought it was a gun, until he realised it was a camera.

Probably just one of the local hard men keeping an eye out, doing a bad Humphrey Bogart, thought Karl.

But there was something disturbing about the man's face. He wasn't hiding it with the pulled-down hat, as Karl first thought; he was *highlighting* it, using the hat to force one's eyes to focus on *that* part of the face, almost as if he wanted to make sure Karl saw it. A large 'Z' stencilled into his face.

Chapter Fourteen

Once when you were only two,
I used to sit right next to you,
I'd guard you bravely as you slept,
And comfort you each time you wept.
Tim Price, *Teddy Bear's Lament*

A chill wind was howling outside the old house, like the lonely ghost of a trapped wolf. Dorothy felt she was drowning in her own shadow in the spreading dark.

The girls huddled under the thin blankets and filthy clothing, neither talking, both shivering. Dorothy was trying to stop her teeth from chattering, but was failing miserably. A couple of times, she tried huddling up beside Tara for some combined body heat, but her attempts were quickly shunned with an elbow directed to the ribs.

Five minutes had passed since Dorothy's last overture to secure some body heat. This time she would be a bit craftier. She eased over stealthily towards Tara's body. She could feel the heat, even though a couple of inches divided them. Then, disaster. Her leg touched Tara's.

'*Arghhhhhhhhhhhhhhhhh!* That's sore. Why'd you nip me in the thigh, Tara? I was only trying to keep warm.'

Tara trained her eyes upward, not even deigning to glance in Dorothy's direction.

'Don't *ever* touch me. I don't like to be touched – by anyone. It creeps me out. Make the same mistake again, and you won't get off so easy, with just a little nip.'

'Can…I at least get the bear, and hold it? *Please*. Can I?'

Tara rolled her eyes. 'As long as it stops you yakking for a few minutes, get it from the mattress.'

Dorothy scuttled up the mattress, found the hole, removed the bear, and scuttled quickly back in from the freezing air. Under the blanket, she kissed the bear and hugged it tightly.

'I can't believe you're kissing that old thing. I saw a rat pissing on it, a couple of nights ago.'

'You're only saying that to be mean. Isn't she, Mister Bear? You'll keep us safe, won't you, Mister Bear?'

'You probably believe that, don't you?' Tara replied, sarcastically.

'Things happen when you believe. That's what my mum always says.'

'Well, isn't your ma the smart one? Bet she's as thick as you.'

'My mum isn't thick. Why are you so mean? I'm not talking to you any more.'

'Best news I've heard since you came here.'

Ten seconds went by.

'Where did you find the bear?'

'Thought you weren't talking to me? If you must know, it was hid behind a hole in the wall.'

'What's its name?'

'Name? You really are a kid, aren't you? How the hell would I know? There's something scribbled on its left paw, but the letters are faded. "King", or something like that. I couldn't make it out too well. Probably the name of the stupid kid who owned it a million years ago.'

Dorothy began scrutinising the paw. 'I can see it, some sort of name. Not King. Kang…? Kinl? No. Ka…Karl! That's his name: Karl…'

Chapter Fifteen

Every man has his secret sorrows which the world knows not;
and often times we call a man cold when he is only sad.
Henry Wadsworth Longfellow

Night. Karl. Walking in slow motion. Fog everywhere. In the distance, a large Victorian house looms, penetrating the miasma like in an old Hammer horror movie. The house will devour him, swallow him in one gulp. His heart is beating so hard it hurts his ribcage. He tries to stop walking, but the house's magnetic grip keeps pulling him in.

I don't want to go there. Please…someone…help…

His shoes start tripping him. Too big. He kicks them off, and continues onwards like a zombie. The house is getting bigger and bigger, his fear more acute. Trousers start slipping from his waist. He almost stumbles over them as they slide down his legs. Wiggles out of them. Followed by his underwear. The coat he's wearing feels like a large gorilla straddling him. It pulls away from him like a leaf in autumn. To his embarrassment, he is now completely naked, but bizarrely getting smaller, thinner.

A child.

Help me…please…someone. But it's not his deep, baritone voice he hears pleading. It's a squeaky, pubescent echo of anxiety and panic.

Closer. The house comes closer. Its shadow reaching out to him. Threatening to grab.

Please…

His hand touches the door handle. He turns it. Involuntary. Door opens. A tidal wave of blood is unleashed like water into a sinking ship. Fills his mouth with the taste of iron and dry cotton. He's gagging. Choking. Drowning.

The bloody tide pulls him inside. A body floats by. His mother. Naked. Dead. Her skin shredded. He reaches for the body. Pulls himself on to it. Like it's a bloated surfboard. Holding on for dear life. Gripping her spongy breasts. His face rests in her face. The stench of her rot is nauseating. Her eyes are open. Overripe with horror.

Reflected in her pupils is a scene, like an old-time movie projector, flipping instantaneous movements of reel. Blurs slowing down towards an understanding of time and object.

He looks deeper and deeper into the eyes. Directly behind his mother, a man stands, naked, bloody knife in hand, laughing. He resembles a centaur but in pig form, draped in a butcher's bloody apron. He mounts her, his corkscrew cock excited and rigid, ready for entry into her vortex.

Noooooooooooooooo! Karl is screaming, but no ears are listening.

Behind the man, lurking in shadows, two young girls point their fingers accusingly at Karl. Blood is dripping from the tops of the tiny fingers. The drops parachute towards the ground, hitting it in slow motion, forming the words, *You let him murder us, you did nothing to stop him...*

Noooooooooooooooooooooooooooooooooooooooooooooooo!

'Karl! Karl, wake up!'

'Huh...? What...?' Karl blinked a few times. His mouth tasted like dusty glue. Brow damp with sweat. Chest heaving.

'You were having a nightmare,' Naomi said, her worried face hovering over his. 'You screamed out a few times. You okay?'

'Yes...' He forced a grin. 'No more cheese sandwiches before bed, ever again.'

'What was it about?'

'Nothing...just the usual crap, being chased through a forest by a strange-looking woman with a bloody axe in her hands. I think it was Lynne, looking more money from me.' He eased out of bed. 'Need to take a leak.'

In the bathroom, he looked in the mirror. Barely recognised the man staring back. Threw cold water on face, before checking hands. They were trembling.

Sneaking a peek out the bathroom door, he tiptoed across the landing to where his coat dangled from a coatstand. Shoved his hand in the inside pocket. Rummaged. Found the pills. Removed two from their enclosure, and tried popping them into his mouth. Missed. Watched in horror as they bounced onto and into the carpet.

'Damn it!' He fell to his knees, fingers fine-combing the plush carpeting.

'Karl? You okay?' Naomi called from the bedroom.

'Yes…just a second.' His fingers frantically searched. Bingo! One recovered. *Where's the other bastard?*

'Karl…?'

'Coming…' He swallowed the sole survivor and headed back to the bedroom.

'You sure you're okay?' Naomi said, concern traced across her brow as he eased back into bed.

'Nothing a hug won't cure.'

Naomi patted her side of the bed. 'Come here, big lad.'

Karl slid over, curving into her, loving her womanly smells, the warmth of her breasts, the beat of her heart against his ear. But more than all these things combined, he loved her protection. He needed that more than anything else at this moment.

Silently, he prayed to a god he did not believe in, not to let him fall asleep.

Not to let the bogeyman get him…

Chapter Sixteen

A gambler is nothing but a man who makes
his living out of hope.
William Bolitho

Friday lunchtime, Karl was just leaving the office to place a quick bet on a sure-thing, impossible-to-lose horse, when a car pulled up alongside. The driver beeped the horn before getting out. He was youngish-looking, hair combed back in a fashion long gone. Despite his youthful appearance, there was something world-weary in his demeanour, something sad and secretive in his eyes.

'What the hell are you doing, blasting your horn? Didn't you see the sign at the corner?' Karl said, eyeing the young man. 'This is a no-noise zone. I should call the cops. Oh, sorry, I forgot. You *are* a cop, Chambers. So, how's the form, Detective?'

'I need to talk to you, Mister Kane. Urgently.'

'Karl or Kane. Quit the "mister" shit. You sound like a schoolboy talking to a teacher.'

'Okay. Kane it is. Now, can we have that talk?'

'It'll have to wait. I only have a minute to get this bet down.'

Karl pointed at the William Hill bookie's shop across the street.

'That's okay. I can wait here till you return.'

'I bet you a tenner you can't.' Karl smiled.

'What's that supposed to mean?'

Just then, a female traffic warden appeared.

'Which of you two gentlemen owns this vehicle?' she said, pointing at Chambers' car.

'It's mine,' Chambers said.

'Can't you see the double-yellow line?'

'You don't understand. I'm a–'

'No, *you're* the one who doesn't understand. You can't park here. That's not too complicated to understand, is it?'

Chambers' hand went to his inside pocket, and produced a small brown wallet, containing his police ID. He flourished it to the woman. 'I'm a policeman.'

'Then you should know better than to break the law. Move the car immediately; otherwise I'll have it towed.'

Karl let out a large, loud laugh. 'Belfast doesn't know the meaning of the word "protocol" when it comes to making money.'

A chastised and chastened Chambers got back inside and started the car.

'That's a tenner you owe me, Chambers,' Karl said, making his way quickly to the bookie's.

Ten minutes later, Karl reappeared, tearing up a docket.

'No luck?' Chambers said, standing at the doorway.

'The nag fell at the first hurdle. A hundred quid gone like coal in Hell. And talking of Hell, what sort of little harassment operation has my devious devil of an ex-brother-in-law sent you on?'

'Inspector Wilson has nothing to do with this. He's over in Edinburgh at the moment, on assignment.'

'Good. Hopefully the bastard stays there. Where's that maniacal thug of a side-kick of yours – 'The Priest', the one who gets so much pleasure from confession?'

'Detective McCormack?'

'The very one.'

'He's back in the station. This is an off-the-record meeting.'

'The last time I saw you two together, you were beating the crap out of him with that kung-fu shit of yours, after he assaulted me.'

'Yes, well…that was in the heat of the moment. I shouldn't have done it.'

'I was grateful you did. You saved my neck, while giving his a good chopping. So, what is it you want?'

'Can we go back to your office and talk?'

'So you can eye Naomi? I don't think so.'

Chambers' face flushed slightly. 'This is a friendly visit, Kane. We got a complaint from the Europa. A guest by the name of Graham Butler received a vicious beating, a few nights ago. Apparently, Butler didn't want it disclosed, because of his reputation as a hard man, but when the regular manager returned from some days off, he immediately reported it to us, as required by hotel policy.'

'Long story short?'

'What?'

'Get to the point. I've a hundred quid to get back from Hill Billy.'

'I checked the hotel's CCTV. You were seen clearly on it; you and Miss Sharon McKeever – or Lipstick, as she refers to herself.'

'Is there a crime in that?'

'I suspect Miss McKeever was there for a sexual encounter, as she has–'

'She's an adult. She can do whatever she damn well–'

'Something bad happened in Butler's room, and you were called in to help her. I know the history between you and Miss McKeever.'

'History? What the hell's that supposed to mean?' Karl bristled.

'She saved you from being killed by Peter Bartlett, the assassin. She shot him. That's more than enough for you to be indebted to her.'

Karl looked at his watch. 'Unless you're going to arrest me for assault and battery, I'm going to go back inside and–'

'Graham Butler is a very dangerous individual. He's a

well-known criminal from London's East End. In one of his prettier moments, he killed a rival drug dealer, cutting him up and disposing of the body parts all over London. At the moment, he's suspected of arranging meetings with drug dealers over here, hoping to extend his franchise.'

'A nice chap, then? Look, I appreciate your telling me, and sticking your neck out. I really do. Though I have to admit, I think you're more concerned about Naomi being dragged into it, than you are about my health.'

'Just make sure you avoid him. We're hoping to send Butler back to London, first chance we get.'

'Butler won't come anywhere near me. He didn't look like a stupid man.'

'One other thing. A journalist from the *Sunday Exposé* has been talking to some of the staff at the hotel. Don't be surprised if the newspaper contacts you.'

'I doubt very much they'll contact me. They only like people who'll tell them what readers of their rag want to hear.'

Chambers turned to leave.

'Aren't you forgetting something?' Karl said, holding out his hand.

Chambers looked puzzled. 'What?'

'The tenner you owe me.'

Chapter Seventeen

There will be killing till the score is paid.
Homer, *The Odyssey*

'Do you think God is punishing us for being bad, Tara?'

'I don't believe in God. There was no God to help me at Blackmore.'

'But...everybody believes in God. If you don't, you go to Hell.'

Tara started laughing without laughter in it. 'Where the *hell* do you think we are right now? Perhaps you weren't the good little girl you thought you were, and you've been sent here?'

The words sent a shiver up Dorothy's back. The howls of wind outside were gathering pace, like the staccato of a million bat wings in a cave. She hugged the bear tighter.

'I hate the wind at night. It scares me,' Dorothy said, trying to prevent her teeth from chattering.

'The wind doesn't bother me. It's my friend. Pastor Kilkee was always terrified of the wind. He thought it was Satan coming to get him, to cart him off to the flames.'

'Who's this Pastor Kilkee? You've said his name a few times.'

Tara didn't answer. She seemed to have drifted away on a boat of memory.

'Tara? You okay?'

'He was a bastard.'

'Oh.'

'Yes, a dirty one. Did things to me, to all the girls at Blackmore.'

'What kind of things?'

'Things…dirty things. Kept me locked up, just like Scarman. Until I escaped. Until I…'

'What? Until what?'

'What's the worst thing you ever did?'

Dorothy thought for a moment. 'I…I took money I shouldn't have, from Grandda McMahon before he died. He had a disease called Old Timers, and kept forgetting everything. Every time he handed me money, he would say: "Didn't I just gave you money yesterday, Dorothy?" And I would put on my best wee innocent voice and say, "No, Grandda McMahon, you didn't." Even though he had. I'm so ashamed of doing it now.'

'When did he kick the bucket?'

'Last year. My granny put him in a home, even though he had his own home. I hated Granny McMahon for that. She's not as nice as Granny Reilly, my other granny.'

'Granny McMahon sounds a right old bitch.'

'She can be nasty, when she wants to be. What about you?

What's the worst thing you ever did?'

'The *very* worst thing?'

'Yes.'

Tara smiled. In the splintered dark, her teeth looked almost canine. As she spoke, her voice sounded different, diseased, like an old woman rotting on her deathbed.

'I killed someone. Killed him good and proper. Rammed knitting needles into his eyes, and all the way up into his brain. And I enjoyed every second of pain I gave him…'

Chapter Eighteen

Were there darker provinces of night he would have found them.
Cormac McCarthy, Child of God

Karl made a left turn into the unused back road, slowing the car to a crawl. The old house could barely be seen from the road, camouflaged by overgrown weeds and trees, but he could still picture it clearly in his mind.

For a second, he was tempted to get out of the car, have a sneak peek, but something foreboding kept him inside the vehicle. Quickly shifting gears, he hit the pedal, proceeding onwards.

Less than a minute later, he came to another isolated house, not as large as the first one, but not a league out.

This time, he did exit the car. Walked up the house's gravel pathway. Before he could knock on the door, an elderly man opened it, the shotgun in his hands aiming directly at Karl's chest.

The man was as broad as a barn door, his thick, knotted muscles earned through the honesty of a lifetime of hard farm work. Thick grey hair showed not a hint of thinning, crowning weatherbeaten skin and sincere but shrewd eyes. A fierce-looking Rhodesian Ridgeback sided up to the man.

Karl held his arms up to the sky. 'Is that how you welcome an old neighbour, Francis Duffy?'

The man's ageing eyes scrutinised Karl, from toe to head.

'Who're you, and what do you want here?'

'Karl, Francis. Karl Kane. Don't you remember me, that nuisance kid always pinching your apples? Remember all the boots up the arse you gave me? I still have the boot prints as proof if you want me to show them to you.'

'Karl...?' Francis' face lit up like a million blessed candles. 'Lad, you're a sight for sore *and* old eyes.'

'Can I take my hands down?'

'What – oh! Of course!' Francis laughed, quickly cradling the shotgun. 'Sorry about that. Don't get many visitors, so I'm always wary of strangers at the door.'

'God help any Mormons coming up the path to convert.'

'Come in! Come in, lad!'

'What about the dog? Doesn't look too happy to see me.'

'King? He'll not touch you. Come on.'

As Karl approached, the dog's tail wagged frantically.

'He's not going to bite, is he?'

'Only if I say so. You must be okay. He didn't even growl. He knows good people when he smells them. Even wagging his tail for you. Proves you have a good soul, Karl. He can tell.'

'I can handle dogs.' Karl patted the dog's head. 'Cats? Now, that's a different matter.'

Inside, Francis seated Karl at a table covered with everything from old newspapers to rusted tools prepared for oiling. The room – like most of the house, Karl suspected – was in dire need of a good cleaning and fixing. Ghostly cobwebs and heavy dust covered parts of farming machinery and other odds and ends, stacked against the walls like medieval torture contraptions.

'Would you like a beer, or something stronger, Karl?'

'Unfortunately, I'm driving, so I'm forced to say no.'

'Tea, then? I'm just after having a cup, and the kettle's still hot.'

'I wouldn't mind a coffee if you have it.'

'Coffee…? Well, let me see. I think I have some somewhere.' Francis opened a cupboard and began searching. 'I've no use for the stuff myself.'

Karl looked about the room, saddened by its declining state. Francis' late wife, home-proud Nora, would be turning in her grave if she could see the state of the place.

'Many a great breakfast I had at this table, Francis. No-one made breakfast like Nora. Could choke a bull, the breakfast she made.'

Francis' eyes brightened at the mention of Nora's name.

'Isn't that the truth, lad? She always had a fondness for you. Looked upon you as the son we never had, especially after Julia was…' He turned and looked at Karl. 'Sorry, lad…didn't mean to bring the past up about your mother.'

'That's okay. Time has softened Mum's passing. I've learned how to cope with the darkness of that time,' lied Karl, his gut tightening.

'Ah! Found it,' Francis said triumphantly, pulling out a dated and grime-encrusted jar of Nescafé, before hitting a switch on a battered kettle housing a small quantity of dull-ish water. 'I knew I had coffee somewhere. A bit out-of-date, I'm afraid. I rarely venture into the village these days – or anywhere else.'

'Don't worry about that. I'm sure it'll taste fine.'

'What way do you take it?'

'Black, no sugar.'

'John Wayne style, eh? How's Cornelius keeping? I haven't heard a thing about him over the years.'

'He's…fine. No, actually, he's not. He's in a nursing home.'

'A nursing home…?' Francis turned and looked sharply at Karl. He seemed on the verge of saying something judgemental, but instead just banged down on the hardened coffee before scraping some lumps out into a cup.

'He's got Alzheimer's, Francis, and it's steadily worsening.'

'Dear Lord…I'm truly sorry to hear that, Karl.' Francis shook his head. The kettle bubbled. He poured the hot water onto the hardened clots of coffee.

'You can only play the hand life gives you,' Karl ruminated.

'Alzheimer's was always my biggest nightmare. I would hate to end up in one of those so-called nursing homes, someone having to wipe my arse. You read the papers, and some of the things they do to people in those places. Horrible…'

'Those are the bad apples you find in every profession. I have to say, he's been well taken care of where he is.'

'Still, there's no place like home, is there?'

Karl felt his face tighten. 'I tried getting him to move in with me, but he almost started World War Three. Wouldn't hear of it.' *Why the hell does that sound like an apology?*

'That day ever comes for me, Karl, it's the shotgun to the auld head. Sugar? Oh, you already said no sugar. God, I hope that's not the first signs of it for me, losing my marbles.' Francis laughed nervously. Handed Karl the coffee, and then sat down opposite.

Karl took a sip of the liquid.

'How's the coffee, Karl?'

Horrible. It tasted of engine oil and damp sawdust. 'Lovely.' He tried not to make a face.

'Didn't I hear something about you a while back on the radio? You were shot at by some religious nutcase?'

Karl nodded, pretending to sip contentedly on the coffee. He put the cup down, hoping Francis wouldn't spot that it had hardly been touched.

'The scumbag's name was Peter Bartlett. He'd killed a few people before getting to me. Thankfully, I had a little guardian angel watching my back, and she killed Bartlett before he killed me.'

'Dear Lord above! The madness out there is unbelievable. But I thought the radio said your brother-in-law, that police-man – what's his name? – saved you?'

'Wilson. Some hope of him saving me. Anyway, he's now my *ex*-brother-in-law. I was divorced a few years back.'

'Divorced…I'm sorry to hear that, Karl.'

A silence sat between them, like an uninvited guest. Karl glanced about the room, feigning interest in pieces of furni-ture. Francis looked at Karl feigning interest, and decided to break the excruciating silence.

'You still haven't told me the reason for your visit.'

'Oh, I was just in the area, to be honest. Thought I'd drop in, see how you're doing.'

'Checking out your old homestead, around the corner?'

'It's no longer ours. I just wanted to have a last look at it. Finally managed to sell it, last week.'

'You've sold it? That house has been in your family for gen-erations.'

'I know, but it was becoming a money pit. I had to sell to the bank, to help cover Dad's medical bills, plus the money for staying at the nursing home. It doesn't come cheap.'

'Bankers are the lowest bastards of the lot. I'd shoot every last one of them dead, then hang them for good measure. The number of livelihoods they've destroyed, and not one of them ever sent to prison.'

'That's how the world has always been, Francis. One law for

the poor, another for the rich. They're just more blatant about it now, there's little shame in any of them. Almost a badge of honour to screw the little guy.'

'Your father worked all his life. When I know I'm heading out the door feet first, I'm going to drink everything I've got, and burn this house to the ground. I'll not let the bastards get their soft hands on a penny of *my* hard-earned money.'

Karl shrugged his shoulders. 'The old house was just rotting away. I never had any intention of living in it. Too many bad childhood memories. At least it ended up doing some good in the long run, paying Dad's bills.'

'Who bought it? Anyone I know?'

'I don't know. The buyer wanted to remain anonymous. That's how they do things these days. All about avoiding taxes, I suspect.'

'I've been over in the vicinity of the house a few times, mostly to find straggling cows or to hunt down foxes killing the chickens. The last time was just a couple of nights ago. Bucketing out of the heavens, as usual. There was a moment… no, it was nothing.'

'What?'

'Well…probably just my bad eyesight playing tricks, but I thought I saw a light flickering on and off, up in the old boarded-up front bedroom.' Francis shook his head. 'There was a lot of lightning that night, so that's probably all it was.'

Karl looked at his watch, then stood. 'I guess I should be going, Francis. Got to get back to work.'

'Don't you want some more coffee?'

'Er, no…I try to limit myself to one cup a day. It was great seeing you again, Francis.' Karl stuck out his hand, but to his surprise, Francis hugged him as if he were the prodigal son.

'Karl…I'm sorry…you know…' Francis said, easing away from Karl.

'Sorry? For what?'

Francis hesitated for a few seconds before continuing. 'That dreadful night. For not being there, to save you, your mother. If only I had looked out my window that night and–'

'It had nothing to do with you, Francis. You have nothing to be sorry about.'

'I should've heard you both screaming. Something…'

Karl forced a smile. 'You'd have needed ears like Steve Austin.'

'Who?'

'*The Six Million Dollar Man*. Anyway, you're not to think like that – ever. If Mum were alive, she'd give it to you for thinking such nonsense.'

Francis nodded sadly. 'You're right. Of course you're right. Just a silly old man with silly thoughts. Guilt can do strange things to the mind. I know Cornelius never forgave himself either.'

'Well, being away at sea, there was little he could have done.'

'Sea? But he…' Francis' words stopped dead. He looked like he had just swallowed a worm. Or opened a can full.

'What? What were you going to say, Francis?'

'Nothing…not a thing…'

'You were going to say *something*. What was it?'

'I…just thought you knew…about Martha Johnson, that's all.'

'Martha Johnson?' Karl thought for a second. 'Didn't she used to own the grocery story in the village, up until a few years ago, before her death?'

'Yes…'

'What about her?'

'Look, Karl, things happened years ago, and you shouldn't be too judgemental about…well…'

'About?'

'Well, Cornelius and her. Only a couple of people knew about it. It was kept very quiet, very discreet. He wasn't out flaunting it.'

'Flaunting what?'

'Their…relationship…'

'Are you saying Dad was having an affair?' Karl almost burst out laughing at the thought of it. 'I find that a wee bit…' He stopped talking. His face changed. Revelation hitting home. 'You…you're saying he was…Dad was with Martha Johnson, the night Mum was murdered, that he wasn't at sea?'

Francis looked very uncomfortable. 'I always thought you knew.'

'No. Never even suspected.' Karl smiled a wry smile. 'That's not very good advertising for a private investigator, is it?'

'I'm sorry, Karl. I…'

'Nothing to be sorry for, Francis. Perhaps what you've told me helps to explain a lot of things about Dad.' From his wallet, Karl removed a card and handed it to Francis. 'If you ever want to talk, that's my business card. Call me any time. *Any* time.'

Francis took the card, looked at it, and nodded.

'I will, Karl. I will.'

Karl walked to the door. Opened it. King followed behind Francis. Karl looked at the old man with fondness. 'It was good seeing you again, Francis. Keep yourself safe.'

'Ha! Anyone comes here uninvited, this old shotgun'll leave him looking like a teabag.'

Karl leaned down and patted the dog's head.

'Keep a good eye on your master, King.'

The dog wagged its tail, and barked. Both Karl and Francis laughed.

Francis watched Karl walk down the pathway towards his car. The old man kept watching until the car drove away before going back inside to his loneliness and memories.

Karl drove slowly, turning the things Francis had said around in his head. Not only about Cornelius, but also the house. *I thought I saw a light flickering on and off, up in the old boarded-up front bedroom...*

He stopped the car directly to the side of his one-time home. Getting out, he closed the door very gently, and walked to the front of the big old house. Rain clouds were gathering overhead, suffocating the last remnants of light the sky was squeezing out.

A dilapidated husk, the house was like the discarded corpse of a once-living home. He couldn't help but feel a pang of sadness, despite all the bad memories. The awareness of such a vast expanse of time, long gone, made him reflective and melancholy.

Images spawned in his head. He thought he could hear his mother's voice calling his name. *Karl! Karl, dinner's ready. Hurry in now, before it gets cold!* He could hear laughter, also. It belonged to his father, pushing him on the old wooden swing behind the house; pushing him higher and higher until he could almost touch the roof, and the fat-bellied clouds, on a fine autumn day. A house filled with happiness and wonder. Then it all changed. Forever. His mother's screams, mad, continuous screeches of hellish agony. Knives. Blood. Terror. Rape. Murder.

A boom of thunder exploded above, making Karl edgy. He checked his hands. They were shaking terribly, like the hands of an alcoholic in bad need of a drink.

Tara watched it all from the tiny hole she had carved out, hardly daring to breathe. She wanted to scream out to the man peering up from below, but was frightened Scarman might hear. She yearned for the man to see her tiny finger wiggling in and out of the hole, trying to catch his attention, but it was hopeless. How could he be expected to see such a tiny thing as a finger from so far away?

More thunder cracks erupted, spewing out rain with a vengeance. Tara watched as the man got back inside his car, and slowly drove away. It made her want to cry.

Chapter Nineteen

When the legend becomes fact, print the legend.
Maxwell Scott, *The Man Who Shot Liberty Valance*

Sunday morning. Bedroom. Karl sat at the table, typing his latest soon-to-be-unappreciated manuscript on his beloved Royal Quiet DeLuxe typewriter. Actually, there was little typing being done, but Karl was doing plenty of staring blankly at a blank page. His fingers hovered nervously over the keys, like a helicopter trying to perch on a house of cards.

A couple of times, his fingers landed briefly on the keys, only to quickly pull away, as if touching acid.

'It's like a damn hothouse in here. That heat must be up full blast,' Karl said, more to himself than to anyone in the room. 'The bloody sweat's trickling down my arse.'

Behind him, Naomi sat contently in the middle of the bed, reading a passel of morning newspapers. She was wearing only Karl's shirt, and no panties, something Karl was finding rather distracting.

'Did you say something, Karl?' Naomi finally raised her eyes over the top of the newspaper.

'Very cheeky of you.'

She looked over at him, slightly confused.

'What is?'

'You pretending to be from Donegal when you're actually from Derry.'

'What're you talking about?'

'You, airing your beautiful derriere shamelessly to the world.'

'Is it really beautiful?' She smiled coyly.

'And loyal.'

'Loyal?'

'It follows you everywhere, just like me.'

She giggled. 'You must have writer's block, my love? Want me to unblock?'

'You can start by dumping those rags you're reading, and getting me a nice cup of very hot coffee.'

'I enjoy reading the Sunday newspapers. There's always juicy gossip to be found.'

Karl made a disapproving sound with his throat.

'And the coffee?'

'You didn't say please.'

'*You* didn't have to say please when I went out into the cold and pissing rain this morning, just to get you those juicy rags.'

'True, but you were only expressing your love and deep gratitude for all the things I've done for you.' Naomi returned to reading. She turned a page. Her face suddenly changed. 'Oh! Karl, *Sunday Exposé* have an article about you and Lipstick.'

'What?' Karl said, pushing away from the table.

'It's not a bad photo of you. Especially compared to the one they have of the thug you beat up. He's scary-looking.'

'Never mind that, let me see what the bastards have made up this time. Chambers warned me about this.'

'Chambers?'

'You know who I'm talking about. The lover-boy detective who fancies you.'

'Stop being silly.'

'Am I? Then why are you blushing, just like he did?'

Naomi laughed. Patted the bed coaxingly. 'Sit beside me. I'll read the article to you.'

'I really don't have time for this kind of…but okay.' Feigning reluctance, Karl sat down on the bed, edging over beside Naomi. Her latent perfume and body-warmth tickled his nostrils. He hoped that's not all they'd be tickling before the morning was over.

'"*Is this the man who took on notorious London crime boss Butler?*", says the wee headline.' Naomi cleared her throat, and continued reading. '"*This silhouetted figure is believed to be the man who sorted out one of London's most feared crime bosses, last week at the Europa, according to our inside sources.*"'

'Inside sources, my bollocks. It was that greasy little worm Raymond.'

'"*The notorious London gangster, Graham Butler, was left with a suspected fractured jaw, missing teeth, and a face his own mother wouldn't recognise.*"'

'Can't believe I'm agreeing with this rag.'

'*"Our sources believe they know who this man is, who rescued a young woman, the victim of a brutal assault by Butler. Her mystery benefactor decided to go quid-pro-quo, giving the London thug a good old Belfast justice beating. Police say no charges have been brought, because no one has come forward with a complaint.* Sunday Exposé *hopes the big bad crime boss has learned his lesson about beating up defenceless women in Belfast and elsewhere. Bon voyage back to London, and good riddance."*'

'Let me have a look at the pictures,' Karl said, secretly chuffed at the article not making him the villain for a change.

'I like that photo,' Naomi said, handing over the newspaper. 'Even in blurry silhouette, you can still make out that roguish grin of yours.'

'What roguish grin?' Karl said, flashing his roguish grin. 'Anyway, how about that coffee you still owe me?'

Something wickedly seductive twinkled in Naomi's eyes. 'I've something a lot tastier.'

'You do?'

'Want to see?'

'Depends.'

'On what?'

'Is it hot, and does it come in a cup?'

'*Very* hot, and comes in *two* cups.' Naomi smiled, and slowly began unbuttoning the white shirt of Karl's she was wearing. Next came her black-laced bra, unhooked from the front, leaving her full breasts fully exposed, nipples hardening. 'Irish coffee or café mocha?'

'Irish, of course.' Karl snuggled closer, and kissed the left breast gently and lovingly, before coming up for air. *'Bonne bouche.'*

'I love it when you talk dirty and French at the same time. Whisper more to me,' Naomi whispered in her lover's ear.

Despite the pissing rain and shitty weather outside, things were starting to look sunny for Karl. Very sunny indeed. Of course, in his world, sunshine never lasted very long, before it was chased away by darkness and demons.

Soon he would meet an old demon from his darkest nightmares. The most dangerous demon of all.

Chapter Twenty

I must not fear. Fear is the mind-killer. Fear is the little-death that brings total obliteration. I will face my fear. I will permit it to pass over me and through me. And when it has gone past I will turn the inner eye to see its path. Where the fear has gone there will be nothing. Only I will remain.

Frank Herbert, *Dune*

'**H**ow many Harry Potter books have you read?' Dorothy asked, listening at the door for any movement from Scarman. Her body was freezing – particularly her tiny toes – but the filthy blanket over her shoulders was at least keeping in a modicum of heat.

Tara ignored Dorothy, all the while chipping furtively at the window's wooden undercarriage with the cutthroat. She had been making good progress, but had become frustrated by the harder wood bedded beneath the framework. If she could only gnaw through it, she believed the entire frame would collapse, or a good part of it.

'I've read all of the *Hunger Games* books as well, Tara.'

Tara stopped momentarily. She stared over at Dorothy.

'Do you really want Scarman in here, slapping you about? Or worse…?'

'I was just–'

'*Just* shut the fuck up. That's the only thing you just need to do.'

Dorothy could feel her face reddening at the sting of Tara's barbed tongue. Tears were welling up, but she willed them away. She wouldn't cry any more. Not for this cruel girl.

Dorothy was feeling terribly alone now, more alone than she had ever been. She wished she were back home with her family, away from these two monsters. Yes, *two* monsters, because as far as she was concerned, Tara was as big a monster as Scarman. The fact that she had boasted about killing someone only confirmed this. And smiling that scary smile when she said it.

'*There's someone coming!*' Dorothy hobbled quickly across to the mattress, the metal leash attached to her ankle almost tripping her over. She quickly spread the blanket out before tunnelling under it.

Tara was momentarily stunned, haphazardly trying to cover up her work at the window. Just at the sound of the door's bolt clanging open, she hit the mattress, shoving the cutthroat inside, leaving no time to slip her foot back into the manacle.

Beneath the blanket, Dorothy's hand gingerly reached out to Tara.

Tara quickly pushed it away.

The door creaked open, and the room filled with heavy breathing, raw with bestial menace.

Dorothy's hand crawled back to Tara's. This time, however, Tara took the hand, squeezing it hard in punishment. Dorothy bit down on her lip, trying not to scream out loud.

They listened as soft footsteps walked across the bare floor. Socked feet? Bare? They stopped at the mattress.

The two girls became statues, not daring to breathe. Dorothy's stomach tightened. Nerves were roiling about inside. She needed desperately to go to the toilet. She silently prayed to God, not for rescue, just don't let her crap herself on the mattress. Tara would kill her. *Really* kill her.

Floorboards creaked. The sneaky footsteps moved off towards the window. There was tapping on the window frame.

Then silence. Tormenting long silence.

Dorothy's heart was hammering so loudly, her head began thumping. *What if he can hear my heart beating so loudly? Is he standing there, grinning, knife in hand, ready to–*

Bang!

The slamming door shattered the deadly silence, making both girls jump. They lay there, not moving, not saying a word, not knowing if Scarman stood there, waiting for them to make a sound.

God had been good to Dorothy. She hadn't crapped herself, but she dreaded what Tara would do, once she found out she had peed herself instead.

Chapter Twenty-One

I must complain the cards are ill shuffled
till I have a good hand.
Jonathan Swift

Swirls of smoke filled Buster McCracken's living-cum-poker room, where Karl and a few associates sat studying the cards Lady Luck had handed them. The group chomped and sucked merrily on large, *Juan Lopez* Cuban cigars, provided by Buster, a seller of all things dodgy and illegal. Everyone in the room seemed impervious to the lung-destroying haze issuing from their mouths.

To Karl's left, Marty Harrington, proprietor of a chain of funeral parlours in the city – Heavenly Harrington's – placed a tidy sum of money in the centre of the table.

'It'll cost you gentlemen another hundred,' Harrington said, before inhaling on his cigar, sending smoky doughnuts floating into the air. He was smiling like a dog with two dicks.

'You must have five aces,' Karl said. 'That's the only time you make a bet that big.'

'Only one way to find out, isn't there?'

'Too rich for a poor boy like me, members of the jury,' said Henry McGovern, a criminal lawyer with a reputation bordering on criminal, and Karl's legal advisor. 'I'll sit this one out and plead no contest.'

'I'll leave the bloodletting to you two,' Buster said, standing, before walking towards the fridge.

Karl sucked on the cigar, cradling the smoke in his mouth. Needled his eyes across the table at Harrington. Harrington tried returning the look. Failed miserably.

'Is this a staring-out contest, Kane, or are you going to play?'

'You look nervous, Marty. The last time I saw you this nervous was at Jimbo Cassidy's funeral, last year, when you had to buy a round of drinks for the mourners. I thought you were going into cardiac arrest.'

'That's a load of balls. Everyone knows I pay my way, and generously into the bargain.'

'Yes, you'd give a poor man the sleeves of your waistcoat. And talking of balls, I went into the chemist yesterday for some deodorant, and the lady behind the counter asked me, "Is it the ball-type deodorant you want, sir?" I looked straight at her and said, "Good God, no! It's for my underarms!"'

Everyone in the room let out a polite laugh, with the exception of Harrington.

'C'mon. Stop stalling, Kane. We haven't all night. Are you in or out?'

Karl looked at his cards. They were shit. Liquorice Allsorts.

Not even a measly pair of deuces. Removing the cigar, he smiled, placed some notes in the centre of the table. 'Make it an even two hundred.'

Harrington almost choked on his cigar. Looked at his cards. Two pair. Threes and fours. Glanced at his dwindling stack of money. Glanced back over at Karl's face.

'You're bluffing, Kane.'

'Only one way to find out. Dig into those long pockets of yours, where you have hamsters performing tricks.'

After a tense twenty-second standoff, Harrington sighed and threw his cards down in defeat.

Karl pulled the winnings over to his side of the table.

'What'd you have?' Harrington asked, looking disgusted with life.

'That sort of information will cost you two hundred to find out, my funerary friend. Next time, be courageous in lieu of timorous.'

'Who wants another Harp?' Buster asked, tray full of beers in hands.

'Nothing stronger?' Karl asked.

'That's what fell off the back of this week's lorry,' Buster said. 'Next week, could be brandy – or bottles of Evian.'

'I was reading about you in last week's *Sunday Exposé*.' Harrington said to Karl, while taking a beer from Buster. 'Still think you're a teenager, showing off to all the girls?'

'As your lawyer, Karl, I must advise you not to say anything that might incriminate you,' Henry said, smiling. 'That may or may not have been my client.'

'Well? Are you going to tell us what it was all about, or not?' Harrington persisted.

'Nothing *to* tell. You know that bloody paper, makes it up as it goes along. If it doesn't fit, they dig a hole and bury it. A bit like your profession.'

'You beat the crap out of some crime boss from England. Are you out of your head or something?'

'Or something…' Karl took a slug of beer. Glanced at his watch. 'Can we change the subject?'

'Provided you're not thinking of running home with all the winnings? We all know Naomi wears the trousers, but it's only a little after midnight, so why don't you give her a call and ask for permission to stay out another hour?'

Good-natured laughter came from Buster and Henry.

Karl smiled. 'If you keep playing the way you're playing, you'll be going home *without* trousers.'

More laughter. Louder.

Scooping up the cards, Karl shuffled, then darted them out to the four corners of the table.

'This is going to be the start of my comeback,' Harrington said.

'On a serious note, Marty, I need some information.'

'Concerning?'

'Along with ordinary burials, you do a lot of cremating, right?'

'Roughly forty percent of my business is done that way now, and it's increasing each year. People are less squeamish about it nowadays. It's funny though, the way Belfast people think. They're dead, but they still shudder at the thought of having their bodies burnt. Maybe they think it's a precursor to where they're going.'

Harrington grinned. Karl was reminded of Dracula.

'Is it possible for a body to be totally incinerated? Gone, into thin air?' Karl asked.

Harrington shook his head. 'Not even in a high-powered furnace. The average person leaves behind six to nine pounds of ash, depending on body frame, weight, *et cetera*. Perhaps a newborn baby's body could totally vanish, because the bones haven't yet matured or become very dense, but I've never actually seen that happen.'

Buster quickly cut in. 'Any chance of hitting all this morbid talk on the head, Burke and Hare? It's starting to give me the creeps, especially talking about babies like that.'

'Why're you asking me all these questions anyway, Kane?' Harrington asked. 'Working a case?'

'Yes, and from what you've told me, I've come to a dead end.'

Chapter Twenty-Two

If you come back in here, I'm going to hit you with so many rights, you're going to beg for a left.
Chuck Norris, *Invasion, USA*

Monday morning, Karl pulled up outside the Naughton house shortly before noon. No work had commenced yet on the devastated shambles across the street that had once been the Reilly home.

A gusty wind was blowing dust and brown sand everywhere. A group of kids in the street thought it was great, being chased by the Brown Blustery Banshee, screaming their heads off each time the wind gathered momentum.

Karl exited the car, head down, and fast-paced to the Naughton's front door. Just as he was about to knock, the door opened.

'I recognised the sound of your car pulling up, Karl. Come on in,' Tommy said, smiling, practically pulling Karl into the hallway, out of the blustery dust. 'Theresa's out visiting her sister, but let me get you a coffee.'

'Hold the coffee, Tommy. I can't stay long. Just came by to let you and Theresa know, I didn't find anything out of the ordinary with regards the deaths of your daughter and family. I asked a few experts, and they all came to the same conclusion, practically. I'm truly sorry.'

Tommy looked crestfallen.

'Theresa'll be devastated to hear that. We did try, didn't we, Karl?'

'You did. You did everything you could, and more.'

Tommy held out his hand and Karl shook it.

'Thank you, Karl, for everything. You're a gentleman.'

'I don't know about being a gentleman, but if you should hear of anything, *anything* at all, you've got my card. Take care of yourself, Tommy. Give my best to Theresa. And stay safe.'

'Well? How'd it go?' Naomi asked, as Karl walked into the office, taking off his coat, almost an hour later.

'Only Tommy was home when I called. He still had that look of guilt, but hopefully my words went some way to ease it. Any calls while I was out earning a crust?' Karl began opening the morning's mail, parked in a wire tray atop the desk.

'Three calls. Two of them sounded quite lucrative. One was from a company boss in Lisburn. Here are his details and queries.' Naomi sat on the edge of the desk, and handed Karl two typed-out pages. 'The other was from a lady who reckons her husband is cheating, and wonders would you investigate it for her?'

'You know I don't do that sort of sleazy stuff. I'm a professional.'

'She lives on the Malone Road, and is quite wealthy.'

'How wealthy?'

'Very.'

'Why didn't you say that? I can always make an exception.'

'The third call was from a man claiming his landlord is slowly poisoning his goldfish, just to get him out of his flat. I told him to either drop by or call back later in the afternoon.'

'Is this what I've come to? Fishy clients carping about bloody goldfish?'

The chime to the outside office door jingled. Through the frosted glass from the office, Karl saw a shadow come in and sit down in the reception.

'Hopefully, that's not the one with the goldfish. I'm not in the mood to listen to a lonely man's paranoia. I can do that any time by talking to myself.'

'Stop being so uppity. That's our bread and butter you're talking about.'

'I'm well aware of that, but I'm the knife who has to carefully slice the bread and spread the butter, sorting time-wasters from genuine clients. So, I *can* get all the *uppity* I like. Now, if you don't mind?' Karl indicated with his chin towards the reception.

Naomi lifted her ample arse off the desk, and headed out the door. Karl reached over and extracted a couple of opened letters in the messed tray.

'Dear Lord, give me strength this day…' Karl sighed, running his eyes over the letters. 'Bloody bills. Relentless torture.'

A few seconds later, the door opened. Naomi popped her head in.

'It's a Mister Carlisle. Needs to talk to you. Face looks messed up pretty ugly.'

'Pretty ugly? That's a paradox. What's he want?'

'Says he's hoping for help in locating a missing person. Shall I show him in?'

'You explained of course that we normally don't see anyone without an appointment, because of how busy we are?'

Naomi folded her arms. 'I'm not in the *mood* to go along with your charades, right now.'

'You just keep that attitude up, and see what happens, Miss Ungrateful. Give me a few seconds, then send him in.'

Karl quickly picked up the phone's receiver, pretending to talk into it, just as the man walked in.

'No, I'm sorry Mayor, but right now I can't take any new cases for at least a month or…' Karl's voice trailed off. He replaced the receiver and glared at the man standing before him. 'I didn't recognise you with your clothes on.'

'Didn't think you'd see me if you knew who it was.' Graham Butler sat down on a chair opposite. His face was ballooned, patterned in black-and-blue. His left eye was totally closed by hyphens of stitches, and his out-of-kilter nose had an enormous sticking plaster plastered to it.

He looked dreadful.

Karl looked pleased.

'And there's me telling the cops that you wouldn't be stupid enough to come looking for me. Now, what's this bullshit about a missing person?'

From an inside pocket, Butler removed a large envelope. Opened it. Produced the clipping from *Sunday Exposé*. Slid it across the desk.

'Good looking guy, if you don't mind me saying,' Karl said, holding the clipping in his hand. 'Looks the type you really wouldn't want to fuck with.'

'You have to forgive my ignorance. I didn't know who you were until one of my associates showed me this. Now you have no place to hide, mate.'

'Hiding? Who's hiding? The only hiding I remember is the one I gave you, *mate*.'

Butler's face did an almost imperceptible nervous twitch, but Karl spotted it.

'You Irish have a saying, Kane: Every dog is brave on his own doorstep. Describes you perfectly. There'll be a time you'll face me on equal terms, not sucker-punching or when I'm naked and defenceless.'

'There's another part of that old saying you forgot to mention.'

'Oh? What's that?'

'Only a stupid dog *leaves* its own doorstep.'

Butler tried to smile, but it was painfully obvious he was in great pain.

'In a strange way, I like you, Kane. You've got balls.'

'As big as a fridge. More than I can say about yours. But tell you what, you end up in one of our jails over here, you'll eventually end up with an extra pair of balls dangling from your arse.' Karl pointed at the door. 'Now, if you don't mind, I've got to see a man about a goldfish.'

'If this were London, you'd be dead by now.'

'In all honesty, I wouldn't be seen dead *in* London. I was courteous to you in the hotel. So-called men beating up defenceless young girls, doesn't go down too well over here in Belfast. It sparks something dark in our psyche. Something that demands blood. If I were you, I'd think myself lucky that all I got was a jolly good kicking, old chap. Want some good advice for free? Get on the next plane home.'

'I'm not going home for at least two more weeks. Maybe longer. For your information, I've a couple of gentlemen outside, waiting in a car. They wanted to come in here, smash the place up, put you in hospital. Perhaps even worse. But I said no, Karl Kane is a smart man. Someone I can do business with. Am I right or am I right?'

'Wrong. On both counts. And as far as you having *two* gentleman in your car?' Karl leaned over the desk. Stared directly into Butler's eyes. 'This is *my* kingdom you're visiting. A simple phone call and I'll have *forty* not-so-fucking-gentle gentlemen busting their balls to return the many favours I've done for them over the years, keeping them from going to prison.'

Butler shook his head in disbelief. 'Okay, have it your way, but that little whore has a very expensive watch belonging to me. It's–'

'If you use the word "whore" again, I won't be responsible for where my fist–'

'–Patek Philippe. It holds a lot of sentimental value in my heart, not to mention its price tag of sixty thousand quid.'

Karl almost swallowed the desk.

From his pocket, Butler removed another envelope, and slapped it loudly on the desk. Karl saw the gun parked in a holster beneath Butler's armpit. It was a deliberate flash from Butler, to let Karl know he wasn't messing about.

'I'm a fair man, Kane. There's a thousand quid in there. See that the little…see that she gets it, along with this message: She has forty-eight hours to return what doesn't belong to her. Otherwise…' Butler stood. 'Well, you fill in the blanks. I'm sure you remember where I'm staying? See you soon, Kane, one way or the other.'

Karl waited until Butler left the room, before making his way upstairs. Rapped on the door of the spare bedroom.

'Who is it?' came the voice of Lipstick.

'Me. Are you decent?'

'I'm always decent. You know that.' She giggled. 'Come in.'

Karl opened the door, and peered inside. Lipstick was sitting up in bed, a copy of Naomi's *Glamour* magazine in her tiny hands. Her face was healing a hell of a lot better than Butler's.

'How're you doing, kiddo?' Karl said, forcing a smile.

'Feeling really great.'

'Really?'

'Really.'

'This is for you.' Karl placed the envelope on the bed.

'What is it?'

'A thousand quid, apparently.'

'A thousand…?' Lipstick hungrily tore the envelope's stomach, spilling out its contents. 'Where…where'd all this come from?'

'A nasty piece of work named Butler.'

'Butler…?' Lipstick's face paled slightly. 'How…how did he know I was here?'

'He doesn't. Not yet, anyway. He's on a fishing expedition at the moment, only instead of a teeny-weeny hook at the end of the line, he's got a bloody humongous harpoon under his armpit that would scare the shit out of Moby-Dick.'

Lipstick pursed her lips. 'What does he want?'

'Playing coy isn't going to cut it, Lipstick. He wants his outrageously expensive watch back. *That's* what he wants.

He's sentimentally attached to it, apparently. Sixty-thousand quid worth of sentimentally.'

'What will we do, Karl?'

'*We?* Ha! *We* will do nothing. But *you*, on the other hand, need to return the watch. This thug isn't going away until he gets it, and within forty-eight hours, starting two minutes ago.'

'I'm not giving it back.'

'I suspected that.'

'And I'm keeping the money.'

'I suspected that, too.'

'Well? Aren't you gonna try and force me?'

'I've never tried to force you to do anything. I'm not going to start now.'

'Good, because I'm going to enjoy spending that bastard's money and wearing his watch.'

'Isn't it a bit big for a wee wrist like yours?'

'My wrist is, but not this.' Lipstick poked a leg out from beneath the bedclothes. The watch was attached to her ankle. She began snaking her leg seductively towards Karl. 'What d'you think?'

'What *you* need to think is what could've happened in that hotel room. It was a warning most young people in similar situations don't get. Someone saintly must be guarding over you. But even Saint Karl's patience is limited.'

Karl turned and left, wondering what the hell Butler would

do once he found out he'd have to add a thousand quid to his increasingly expanding *List of All Things Lovely And Lost*?

Downstairs, Naomi waited, arms folded.

'Are you going to tell me what's going on, or do I have to wait and read about it in the papers? That was Butler, right?'

'Right.'

'He was here looking for Lipstick, I take it?'

'Right again. You're good at this.'

'Stop trying to piss me off. You've got to call the police, Karl, tell them he was here making threats to you.'

'How many times do I need to tell you to stop earwigging?'

'If I didn't listen in, I wouldn't know half of what the hell goes on in here at times.'

'Well, this was one of those times when I didn't want you to know.'

'*Are* you going to call the police, or should I?'

'As Frank Sinatra *didn't* say: I'll handle it *my* way. Don't worry. I have ways of dealing with Butler.'

'Yes, I read about those ways in last week's paper.'

'He's threatened Lipstick. You want me to turn my back on the wee girl?'

'For God's sake! Stop with the martyrdom complex! She's *not* a wee girl, she's a woman, fully in charge of her life. You can't keep being her knight in shining armour each time she–' Naomi stopped in mid-flow. Looked over Karl's shoulder. 'Lipstick? What are you doing dressed and out of bed?'

Lipstick smiled. 'I'm fully recovered, Naomi, and raring to go.'

'Go?' Karl said, looking directly at Lipstick. 'I hope you're not thinking of leaving, especially the way things are at the moment?'

'Look…I love you both to death, but I'm not staying to see you argue over me.'

'No one's arguing over you,' Karl said.

'That's right, Lipstick,' agreed Naomi. 'This…has nothing to do with you. We were only–'

'My face has practically healed, and anyway, I've got to get back to work eventually. It took me a long time to build up my clientele list, and I'm not ready to throw that list away – at least not for a couple more years.'

Karl spread out his arms in an appeal. 'C'mon, kiddo. You don't need to go to…work – at least not right now. Wait a couple more days. I promise it'll be sorted.'

'You don't need to sort anything, Karl. As Naomi said, I'm a woman, not a wee girl.'

'I…' Naomi fumbled. 'I only meant–'

'I know what you meant.' Lipstick walked over to Naomi, and kissed her gently on the cheek. 'And you're right.'

'You have Butler's watch,' Karl quickly interjected. 'You could sell it. Surely the money from that could keep you free from working, at least for a couple of years?'

'I'm keeping the watch as a future investment, or for someone *very* special whose birthday is coming up,' Lipstick said, giving Karl a mischievous wink, and then a kiss on the cheek. 'Now, I really must be going. I already have an appointment with a client, a nice one this time.'

Once Lipstick had left, Naomi looked over at Karl, her face filled with guilt. 'That was all my fault, wasn't it?'

'Don't be silly. She was going to leave shortly anyway. If anyone's to blame for this, it's Butler. He started the whole mess.'

'I just hope she'll be okay. If anything should happen to her, I won't forgive myself.'

Karl's face lost its pleasantness. '*Nothing's* going to happen to her. You have my word on that.'

'You're sure?'

'One hundred percent.' Karl kissed Naomi. 'Have I ever let you down before?'

'No.'

'End of conversation.'

Naomi smiled, relieved. 'Okay.'

Karl waited until Naomi had left the room before lifting his mobile from the table. Hit a few buttons. Placed it to his ear. Listened to the whispery tone. Once it stopped, a deep, sandpapery voice said: 'Karl?'

'Ciarán. How's things?'

'Couldn't be better. Long time no hear. How's everything?'

'Not too bad. Listen, need to have a wee job done, ASAP.'

'No problem. I still owe you big time for getting me out of that shit with the peelers last year.'

'You won't owe me anything after this.'

'What can I do for you?'

'I saw a rat in the office earlier. Need your skills to make sure it doesn't come back.'

'A large rat?'

'Yes, quite large. Does the John Hewitt suit for a meet-up?'

'Could do with a swallow, now that you've mentioned it.'

'How does two o'clock sound? Most of the afternoon crowd will be drifting out by then.'

Chapter Twenty-Three

Ah! que la vie est quotidienne.
(Oh, what a day-to-day business life is.)
Jules Laforgue, *Complainte sur certains ennuis*

The John Hewitt had been packed with afternoon diners, barflies and the inevitable freeloaders looking for liquid freebies, but, as Karl had predicted, the crowd was now dispersing to greener pastures. The legendary wolf pack of booze-nosed journalists who monopolised the long wooden counter had all but disappeared, leaving only a small hard-core to protect the fort against marauding non-combatant civilians.

Karl sat in the back room, watching the front door, his back against the wall – a habit he had picked up in his card-playing career. He was drinking a glass of water – a sacrilege in the cosy pub and restaurant, but he wanted to keep his head clear.

Just as he glanced at his watch for the umpteenth time, a familiar figure entered through the doors, glancing about.

Stocky, bearded, a well-worn face and wearing a cut-off sheepskin jacket, Ciarán Murphy looked every inch the fierce mountain man he was. Three years ago, Ciarán had been languishing in a prison cell, charged with the murder of a man found with his throat cut in a secluded forest section of the Cave Hill, just outside Belfast. The man, a notorious sex fiend, had raped Ciarán's young daughter, Bronagh.

Fortunately for Ciarán, his wife Greta – a childhood girlfriend of Karl – contacted the PI, pleading for any help he could give. Within days, through his criminal and police contacts, Karl had the information he needed. The only witness against Ciarán, Jimmy Grason, had been a police informer, a fact not disclosed before or during the trial. Grason himself was suspected of having committed sex attacks over the years, but was seen as too valuable an informant for the police to put in jail. The case was quickly dropped.

Karl raised his hand, and Ciarán nodded before threading his way between tables to the back room.

'How's it hanging, Karl?' said Ciarán, sitting down.

'Like that lousy bastard, Albert Pierrepoint. What're you having?'

'I wouldn't ignore a pint of Harp if someone was kind enough to place it in front of me.' Ciarán smiled, showing more gaps than teeth, a testimony to the many legendary scraps he had been involved in as a bare-knuckle street fighter in the bloody and dirty streets of Belfast.

'How's the family doing?'

'Doing great. Greta said hello. Your own?'

'I haven't heard any of them complaining lately, so I must be doing something right.'

More small-talk ensued until the waiter brought the pint of Harp. Ciarán made half of it disappear in a two-second gulp, while Karl paid.

'Thirsty, were you, Ciarán?'

'Just wetting a parched throat.'

Karl waited until the waiter left before getting down to business.

'This rodent is not your typical run-of-the-mill type. It's dangerous. Very dangerous. I've tried to persuade it to leave – verbally and forcefully – but it's stubborn, to say the least. My way wasn't too effective, I have to admit now.'

'No problem. I'm probably a bit more persuasive than you. Do you want it exterminated, never to be seen again?'

'No. Nothing like *that*. I don't mind the never-to-be-seen-again bit, but not exterminated. Just that it goes back to where it belongs – and stays there, never to darken these lovely shores again with its greasy tail.'

'I'm sure we can come to some sort of accommodation, Karl.'

From his pocket, Ciarán produced a packet of mints and offered the open roll to Karl.

Out of politeness, Karl availed himself of one. It was warm, the heat generated from the pocket nestling close to Ciarán's ballbag. Karl gingerly placed the mint in his pocket, saying he would have it later. He removed an envelope from the same pocket, handing it to Ciarán.

'All the details are in here, along with a few expenses.'

'I don't want any money. I owe you big time.'

'Take it. Get yourself some sleeves for that coat.'

Ciarán grinned. Pocketed the envelope. Finished the remaining beer in one swallow. Stood. Shook Karl's hand. Left the pub. No more words spoken.

Karl made himself scarce a minute later.

Chapter Twenty-Four

Listen, Dundy, it's been a long time since I burst into tears
because a policeman didn't like me.
Dashiell Hammett, *The Maltese Falcon*

Two days later, Naomi was closing for lunch when Detective Chambers, accompanied by Detective Harry McCormack, appeared at the door. A one-time Special Branch member, McCormack was a six-three pillar of brick-shit-house-hard muscle, baptised in the fire of broken-bones, strap-your-balls-on street fights in Belfast. His non-smiling face was as welcome as the Pope on the Shankill Road.

'We waited until everyone had gone, Naomi, so as not to cause a scene.' Chambers sounded apologetic. 'Mister Kane's in, I take it?'

'What's this about?' Naomi demanded, eyeing the duo suspiciously. 'Karl's had a hard day.'

McCormack, chomping at the bit, said, 'My heart bleeds for him. Why don't you just get Kane, and we'll tell *him* what it's all about, girlie?'

'Girlie?' Naomi's face morphed into battle mode. 'Who the hell do you think you're talking to? What's your name?'

'Detective McCormack.'

Naomi nodded with recognition. 'Oh, now I recall. Detective McPiggy. Isn't that what the other officers call you?'

'Huh…?' McCormack looked as if he had just had a dick-caught-in-zip moment.

'For your own good, *Mister*, don't ever make the mistake of patronising me again, unless you want a good kick in the–'

A hand touched Naomi's shoulder.

'*Grrrrrrrrr*. Easy, tiger,' Karl said, making a paw with his fingers before breaking into a wide smile. 'We don't want the big bad detective getting tough with you, Naomi, do we now?'

'Just let him try it!' Naomi glared at McCormack, before walking back in and heading up the stairs.

'You really need to hone your people skills, McCormack,' said Karl, as soon as Naomi had left. 'Or buy a personality for yourself over in Smithfield.'

'We need to ask you some questions, Kane,' Chambers said.

'I'd invite you over to the wee café across the street for coffee, Chambers, but you'd have to leave your guard dog outside, especially one with a face longer than the *Lord of the Rings* trilogy.'

'Here will do fine. It shouldn't take long.'

'Go ahead then. Ask all the questions you want. You mightn't get any answers, though, and you ask them here at the door, not inside.'

'We're inquiring about the disappearance of one Graham Butler. Any information you may–'

'*Whoa.* Hold on a sec. Why're you asking me about that scumbag?'

Chambers pulled out a small notepad. 'According to our information, he was last seen leaving *here*, two days ago. He was to return to his hotel for a meeting, but he never made it.'

'Another one added to your long list, Kane,' McCormack snarled. 'Seems people who cross you either end up murdered or disappear into thin air.'

'If you believe that, shouldn't you be frightened?'

'Frightened, of *you*? God, what I'd give to have you alone for–'

'Detective?' Chambers said softly, but with authority. 'Can you go back to the car, please? I'll finish this report.'

McCormack seemed on the verge of ignoring Chambers' request. Then, thinking better of it, he complied, turning and stalking out the door.

Chambers waited until McCormack had left.

'You don't make it easy for people to like you, do you, Kane?'

'I don't care if people like me or not. I'm not running for election. Now, what is it you want?'

'Is there anything you can tell me, now that Detective McCormack has left?'

'Have you checked out the drug dealers Butler was dealing with? They should be your prime suspects.'

'They *are* the prime suspects. That's why we want to be able to eliminate you from our inquiries, so that we can focus entirely on them, and not waste time elsewhere.'

'Off the record?'

'Okay,' Chambers nodded. 'Off the record.'

'I detested Butler. He was a cowardly thug who enjoyed beating up young girls, and using them for all sorts of depraved things, as well as—'

'Past tense.'

'What?'

'You keep talking of Butler in the past tense.'

'Do I? Wishful thinking, I suppose. Look, to be frank with you, will I lose any sleep, if something appalling *has* happened to the scumbag? No. Do I know where he is? No.'

Chambers stared at Karl for a few seconds before answering. 'I just hope, for your sake, that you're telling the truth. If you remember anything of importance, will you contact me?'

'My birthday's next week. How's that for importance?'

Without answering, Chambers turned and walked towards the waiting police car with a seething McCormack sitting at the wheel.

Karl watched the car drive away, before returning inside. Naomi was sitting in the middle of the stairs, a worried look on her face.

'So, Butler has disappeared, eh?'

'It would seem that way.'

'Is there anything I should be aware of?'

'Not that I'm aware of.'

'Cut the blarney. I'm not in the mood for it. Has this anything to do with me pressuring you about Lipstick's safety?'

'You pressure me? Get real.'

'You were gone for over four hours on Monday night. Where were you?'

'What did I tell you when you asked me that very same question, the next morning?'

'Playing poker with your mates.'

Karl pulled his mobile from his pocket. Hit a button. Walked up the stairs to Naomi. Handed her the mobile.

'That's Henry McGovern's number ringing. When he answers, ask him where I was on Monday night.'

Naomi placed the mobile to her ear. Gazing levelly at Karl, she listened to the tones beeping. Henry's voice suddenly interrupted. 'Karl?'

'Oh, sorry, Henry, this is Naomi. I hit the wrong button on Karl's mobile. Sorry for bothering you. No, everything's fine. Thank you. Sorry again.'

Karl stared at Naomi. She stared back.

'Seeing you didn't ask him, I take it you believe me?'

'Yes…sorry…'

'Can I have my mobile back, please?' Karl put on his hurt

voice, and stuck out his hand. Naomi placed the mobile in it.

'I'm sorry, Karl…it's…it's just–'

Karl kissed her full on the lips, smiled, and said, 'Let's make sure we put this matter to bed, once and for all.'

They walked up the remainder of the stairs, hand-in-hand.

Almost two hours later, Karl and Naomi sauntered back down the stairs, suited and booted in their gladdest of rags. Smiles plastered across their faces, they looked like two kids caught doing naughty things by teacher.

'All that lovemaking has made me very famished, Naomi. I'm really looking forward to this meal.'

'You're becoming very bad, you know, the older you get,' Naomi said, half giggling.

'Bad in a good way, or bad in a *bad* way?'

Naomi purred against his neck. '*Verrrrrry* bad.'

'Well, I want to thank you, Miss Fitzpatrick, for sharing the last couple of hours with me, and for allowing me to boldly go where no man had gone before – at least I hope they haven't.'

'I really don't know what you're talking about, Mister Kane?'

They walked out into the cool air of an unusually tranquil Belfast evening. Karl was always suspicious of peace and quiet in Belfast. It felt as if all the inhabitants were huddling in their homes, plotting something dangerous and illicit. And it always meant one thing coming sooner rather than later: trouble.

Big time trouble.

Chapter Twenty-Five

Clear the air! Clean the sky! Wash the wind! Take the stone from stone, take the skin from arm...
TS Eliot, *Murder in the Cathedral*

The Northern Whig bar and restaurant stands at the corner of Bridge Street, in the heart of Belfast's cathedral quarter. Dominating the opulent interior are three impressive granite statues. Rescued from the Communist Headquarters in Prague after the fall of communism, they depict the muscular socialist proletariat, steadfastly working for the glorious revolution.

While Karl and Naomi sat waiting patiently for their meal in the lavish surroundings, Graham Butler wasn't too many miles away, also sitting.

However, Butler's surroundings weren't so friendly, or filled with ambient music and the mouth-watering aroma of good food. He was completely naked, strapped to a rough wooden chair, surrounded by walls adorned with a forest of photographs and newspaper clippings. He was somewhat unnerved to see his own face staring down at him from the wall, on pages from the *Sunday Exposé* and other newspapers.

PAST DARKNESS

It had been a long, brutal night for Butler. Or had it been night, at all? It was hard to discern between night and day right now. He was sliding in and out of hallucinations, his disorientation caused by fatigue and pain. At times, he thought he was home, in London, at his abode, eating the fine food and expensive wine that he was accustomed to. Then, just as quickly, he was transported to a castle's keep, tormented by some sadistic guard, laughing in his face, forcing him to eat pigswill.

Despite the pain ravaging his body, however, he was still alive – at least for now – and that's all that mattered.

He dearly wished that he had never come to this accursed shit-hole of a city, regardless of how lucrative the prospect had once looked. His photo peering down at him from the wall seemed to be berating him for such negative thoughts, and for the situation he had allowed himself to become entrapped in.*Sitting here wallowing in self-pity isn't going to get you out of this mess. Get off your fucking good-for-nothing ass, and do something – and quickly, before it's too late!*

He began rocking the chair to and fro, all the while expanding and releasing his massive muscles, applying pressure to the fetters compressed against his battered body. The leather straps incised his skin, flaying and burning. He gritted his teeth, trying to block the pain. He felt on fire. He felt cold. He felt dizzy. It was only a matter of time before he passed out with pain once again.

The photo on the wall began laughing at him.

The beam from a small industrial lamp was directed straight into his eyes, forcing him to squint each time he glanced about his surroundings, or tried conversing with the human shadow lurking behind the spotlight's glare. Despite the horrendous heat emitting from the lamp's close proximity, he felt nothing but a chilliness sheeting his skin. 'Can't you shine that fucking light somewhere else, instead of into my eyes?' Butler said for the umpteenth time, and for the umpteenth time he was greeted with dead-man's silence.

Who the hell was holding him captive, and for what reason? To kill him? But why go to all this trouble, when they could simply have shot or stabbed him as he left the Spaniard pub, in the city centre? Was it a rival drug dealer, sending him a message? He hoped to God it wasn't paramilitaries. He'd seen enough in his short stay in Belfast to know what the bastards were capable of. Unthinkable horrors, things even he would shy away from.

He could handle all sorts of beatings, but not much can be done when someone pops a bullet in your head, and dumps your body in the street like a sack of rotten bones for the dogs of Belfast to devour.

However, the survivalist in him wasn't going to allow himself to go to the grave quietly. No fucking way. He'd sent enough men to early graves, without wishing to join them at this stage in his life.

The last thing he remembered was pissing all that lovely Guinness up against a graffiti-scarred wall, in some godforsaken entry close to the holy of holies, Saint Anne's Cathedral.

Even before he had managed to get his cock out to relieve his bloated bladder, he'd been approached by at least three prostitutes – one of whom he suspected of being a male in some sort of bizarre drag – offering to hold his cock for him while they did strange and wonderful things to other parts of his body.

He had declined, reluctantly. The spirit was willing, but his languid fleshy member was weak and feeling woefully ineffective. He was no use with booze in his blood. It always killed his libido.

Something had happened when he was urinating, but what? He tried to remember, to bring his mind back to that very moment. Was it a black out? He'd had a few of those in his time, though none recently. Then it came to him: a Belfast-style blowjob: a powerful blow to the back of the head with some blunt weapon, something flat and heavy.

Now that he thought of it, he could feel the back of his skull throbbing; could sense dry stickiness mapped on his neck. Head wounds always bleed profusely.Re-focusing, he could hear individual noises behind the spotlight. A sinister cornucopia of sounds: something metallic being dragged? Small drawers being slid open? Items being removed from the drawers?

He inhaled very slowly, almost imperceptibly, trying to stretch out the leather straps criss-crossed on his massive chest. There was very little give, but he kept trying. He was sure he was gaining some tiny movement. A fraction. Hope.

His patience wore off again. 'What do you intend doing with me? Eh? Can't you fucking talk? At least be a man and face me, instead of hiding behind shadows, like a wanker.' Silence greeted his demand, infuriating him further. 'For fuck sake, you lousy bastard! Say something – *anything*!'

The spotlight moved a few inches to the left. The glare deadened slightly.

'Sorry about that,' a muffled voice said in the darkness. 'Didn't know it was bothering you so much. My apologies.'

Butler squinted. Despite blue afterglow spots dancing in his eyes, he could now make out the figure of a man, draped in what looked like a scuffed and bloody butcher's apron, a surgical mask covering half his face. The leather apron brought a quick-flash memory to Butler of when he was a lad of fourteen, working in the filthy tannery, waiting for the hides of slaughtered beasts from the nearby abattoir.

'Who the hell are you? What's this all about?'

'It really doesn't make a lot of difference who I am.' Now he could make out the man's unblinking eyes, drilling into his own, as if peering into the brickwork of his soul. 'Knowledge of my name will not change the outcome.'

'What fucking outcome? What the hell's all this about?'

'I need you to answer some questions. Nothing difficult.'

'Are you going to tell me what the fuck is going on?'

'Perhaps in due course. For now, though, you need to accommodate me. Why are you harassing Mister Kane?' The man was now walking around behind him.

Kane? The bastard. He should have known he was behind this, somehow. That cowardly fucker couldn't do his own dirty work.

'What makes you think I'm harassing that scumbucket?'

'Don't answer a question with a question. It's one of my pet hates.'

'*Arghhhhhhhhhhhhhhhhhhhhhhhhhhhhhhhhhhhhhhhh!*'

Butler's left nipple went shooting across the room like a miniature champagne cork. He screamed so loud, the crown works of his teeth rattled in his mouth. His head dropped to his chest, breath caught hard in his throat. *'Fuck! Fuck! Fuck!'*

His hair was pulled back violently, bringing his head back to face the ceiling with a snap.

'Pay attention, Mister Butler.' A small, polished item was held between finger and thumb of the man's hand. He tapped the tip of Butler's nose with it. 'This is a Swann-Morton Number Ten surgical blade. A beautiful piece of singular metal, used for making small and accurate incisions. Be thankful I don't believe in inflicting needless pain. I could have used a pair of rusted pliers, and twisted the nipple off, but I'm not a barbarian – although I can be if pushed.'

Butler gritted his teeth. His eyes bulged like a wild animal pushed beyond endurance.

'Okay, okay. Look, I…we, Kane and me…we had a bit of a run-in. Nothing serious. It…it just got a bit out of hand. That's it, really. Look, I know you're Kane's friend, and you're probably pissed off about me threatening him in his office, but…for fuck sake, I just lost my temper. Nothing came of it. It was just a bit of mouthing from me. That's all.'

'The newspapers reporting the incident in the hotel didn't seem to think it was "nothing serious", did they?'

'Come on! You know those bastards will say anything to sell their rag. A few fisticuffs, and they turned it into an all-out battle. Truth be told, Kane kicked my ass good and proper, and I deserved every bit of it. I was just angry when I went back to his office to threaten him. Stupid macho shit.'

'And you threatened to do what, exactly?'

'It was nothing. Just a bit of messing about – *arghhhhhhh-hhhhhhhhhhhh!*'

The other nipple went flying, bouncing off the lamp's metal face before resting on the floor.

'You don't learn very well, do you, Mister Butler? Don't try diluting the truth with me. I don't like people insulting my intelligence.'

An alarm went off on the man's wristwatch for a few seconds, and then went dead. From a metal table, he picked up a roll of silver duct tape. Sliced a section off with the surgical blade, and secured the tape to Butler's mouth.

'There. You can scream all you want now. We'll recommence our conversation when I return.'

He brought the surgical knife close to Butler's face. Droplets of his blood hung from the glinting surface.

Chapter Twenty-Six

You can never plan the future by the past.
~Edmund Burke, *Letter to a Member of the National Assembly*

At about the same time as Scarman was leaving Butler to his thoughts, Karl was excusing himself from the table, and making a beeline for the toilet. Once inside, he checked the place was empty, before locking the door behind him.

He hit Ciarán's number. Two seconds later, a voice answered at the other end.

'Karl?'

'Ciarán, just calling to say job well done on the rodent.'

'You being sarcastic?'

'What's that supposed to mean?'

'I haven't been able to do anything about it, at least not yet.'

A puzzled look appeared on Karl's face. 'What're you talking about?'

'The rodent disappeared, just as I was setting a trap with some poison in it. One minute it was there, next it was gone.'

'But I've just received news to the contrary.'

'I don't know anything about that. I was going to call you

this afternoon, but I decided to wait another day, just in case it showed up again. I didn't want to disappoint you.'

For a few seconds, Karl stood still. Thinking. Wondering. 'That's…that's okay. No harm done.'

'I'll give you your money back when I–'

'Forget about it. One way or the other, the job's done. We'll talk later.'

Karl clicked the phone off, and stood there digesting what Ciarán had told him. Did Butler leave on his own accord, or had something spooked him? The cops? Rival drug dealers? Or had he fallen foul of the thugs he was hoping to partner with, to extend his empire? Whatever the reason, Butler had left in a hurry, and that was a big bloody Belfast blessing.

The thought cheered Karl right through to the marrow of his bones, as he returned to the table and Naomi.

'What's the big smile for?' said Naomi.

'I needed that. A *load* off my mind.'

Naomi made a face. 'Don't be disgusting. Spoiling the night with toilet humour.'

'You're right. My apologies, my lovely lady,' said Karl, reaching for his brandy. 'Want me to order dessert?'

'No need to. I've got something back in the apartment.'

'You have?' Karl said, trying to sound all-innocent. 'I hope it's something very hot and sticky. That would finish off a very perfect night.'

Chapter Twenty-Seven

*No, no! Don't you touch that, little lamb. Don't touch my knife,
that makes me very mad. That makes me very, very mad.*

Reverend Harry Powell, The Night of the Hunter

Tara was crouched in the darkness, listening at the door.
She hadn't moved in an hour. Cat-like stance.

'Tara?' whispered Dorothy from the mattress. *'What was all
that screaming?'*

No answer from Tara.

Dorothy waited another full minute before trying once
more.

'Tara? What…what was all that horrible screaming? It
sounded like a banshee with its–?'

'Shut up!'

Tara walked away from the door. Stood towering over Dorothy, chest heaving, as if she had run a mile. In the gloom, her
eyes had the intimidating presence of a sawn-off shotgun.

'You can't do anything you're fucking asked, can you, Bucket
Mouth? That mouth of yours never stops.' Tara made her hand
into a mouth. 'Yakkety-yak, yakkety-yak, yakkety-fucking-
yak. On and on and on. Tara this, Tara that. You wouldn't last

five fucking minutes in Blackmore. If the staff didn't fix you, the other girls would do you in.'

'I...didn't mean to upset you. I'm sorry–'

Tara's face began morphing into something, her skin like rubber being melted. It was no longer Tara, but an entirely different person, a Jekyll/Hyde transformation.

She slid up to the end of the mattress, and removed the cutthroat from its hidden niche. Opened the cutthroat, and knelt down beside Dorothy. Placed the blade against Dorothy's neck.

Dorothy felt the cold dullness of steel on her neck. She began shaking. She wanted to scream, but fear locked her tongue. Then, something strange took over. Her body suddenly became light. She was having an out-of-body experience. She seemed to be floating on the ceiling, looking down at the horrific scene, her throat being cut, blood everywhere. Tara was kneeling beside her, laughing that maniacal laugh of hers.

'I warned you about saying sorry. *Didn't I?*' Tara's nostrils flared in and out, breathing more pronounced. Her eyes had lost their pupils.

Dorothy blinked in answer, fearful of nodding with the blade at her neck.

'You think I won't slit your worthless throat?'

Dorothy felt faint. Tears began wetting her eyes.

Tara pierced Dorothy's skin with the blade. A drop of blood

the size and shape of a fish's eye oozed from her neck. It rested on the blade, gleaming in the dull darkness of hopelessness and despair.

The pain was excruciating, but Dorothy uttered not a sound. She stopped breathing, silently praying to God to take her away from this Hell, and Satan's queen imp.

For the longest time, the blade rested on her neck. Then into the room came a soft sound, a mechanical droning, like a million flies with clipped wings: a van's overworked engine.

The sound seemed to waken Tara from her murderous trance. She stood. Closed the blade. Returned it to the mattress. Made her way to the door, once again standing statue-still and listening, as though she had never left.

Dorothy's eyes were closed, lips quivering in a silent entreaty.

At the door, Tara now manoeuvred her hand into the niche, edging her fingers along the lock system. Her index finger touched the bolt. She hooked the finger over the curved metal ending, and eased the bolt from its enclosure, sliding it quietly to freedom. The door opened.

Without another word, or a glance back at Dorothy, she slipped out of the room and onto the shadowy landing, her ears fine-tuned to the tiniest of noises emitting from downstairs.

Chapter Twenty-Eight

God answers sharp and sudden on some prayers,
And thrusts the thing we have prayed for in our face,
A gauntlet with a gift in't.
Elizabeth Barrett Browning, *Aurora Leigh*

Semi-darkness shrouded Hill Street as Karl and Naomi returned from their most enjoyable night out.

Naomi inserted the key and pushed the door open. Karl walked in behind, and was about to close the door when Naomi stopped him.

'What this?' She bent and picked something up off the floor. A small package. She handed it to Karl.

'Why the hell would someone be leaving a package in our hallway?' Karl said, scrutinising the tiny box. His stomach knotted when he saw the labelling.

'What's wrong, Karl?'

He stared at the box, but before he could answer, his mobile rang. Karl glanced at the screen. *Unknown caller.*

'Who's this?'

'Glad you received my little gift, Karl.'

Karl immediately pushed Naomi down the hallway, shielding her, as if expecting a sniper's bullet. Jutting his head out the door, he quickly glanced up and down the length of Hill Street. It was filled as usual with people out for the night, milling about the cafés and pubs, laughing out loud in warm conversations.

'Who the *hell* is this?'

'I'm disappointed in you, Karl. You don't remember?'

'Why don't you refresh my memory?'

'*Who is it–?*' Naomi began to whisper, as Karl placed a finger to his lips, easing her further down the hallway, covering the phone with his hand.

Then Karl was out of the door, slamming it behind him. He began pacing up the street, his eyes darting left and right. He placed the mobile back to his ear.

'What do you want?'

'You're heading in the right direction, Karl,' said the voice at the other end. 'That's right. Keep walking. You're getting warmer, though you look warm already in that lovely overcoat. You do look *very* dapper this evening.'

Karl tried to keep his breathing steady.

'What is it you want? Hello? You still there?'

'Still here, Karl. And you're still there. It won't help, you know, using the shadows to try and camouflage yourself. Very good though, very sneaky of you, Mister all-grown-up-now PI. But what makes you think I'm in the street?'

Karl shifted his attention to the brightly lit glass-walled rooms of the University of Ulster, up ahead. On the ground floor of the building, a café was filled with silhouettes, moving in wavy slow motion.

'Why don't you join me in the café?' Karl said, quickening his pace. 'We can have a wee chat about–'

The phone went dead. Karl watched for any unusual movement from the café: someone walking fast, door slamming, car speeding away. But there was nothing. Nothing but heavy darkness and heartbeats bouncing about in his skull. Naomi! He made his way quickly back to the office.

'What was all that about?' Naomi said, as Karl bundled in through the door, his face drained.

'Not a thing. Shadow-chasing.' Karl looked suspiciously at the package resting on the table. 'I suppose it would be ridiculous to call the bomb disposable people?'

A look of horror appeared on Naomi's face. 'You don't think it's a–?'

'Of course not.' Karl said, his voice filled with uncertainty. 'I'm just winding you up.'

'Don't, because this isn't funny.'

'Just to be on the safe side though, why don't you go across the street?'

'Don't talk nonsense.'

'Just in case. Please.'

Naomi looked at the package, and then at Karl, before

walking, still grumbling, out the door.

'Wish the hell I had a cig...' Karl mumbled, while probing the box with his pen, flipping it over from side to side. Gingerly, he began opening the package, as if it *were* a bomb waiting to explode in his face. 'What the hell...?'

Inside the cardboard, a small, see-through Glassine plastic sleeve. He eased it out. A small opaque shadow could be seen contained within the sleeve. Holding it up to the light, he scrutinised its contents. It looked like old crumpled paper, its edges bordered with burgundy. 'A double-headed mermaid?' Then it struck him. He knew what it was. More importantly, he knew where he had last seen it. 'Oh shit...'

'What is it?' Naomi asked.

'For God's sake, Naomi! Thought I asked you to go across the street.'

'You actually thought I was scared of a bomb, after living here for almost a decade?'

'That doesn't give you the right to sneak the hell up on me like that.'

'Out-sneaking you seems to be the only way to get to the truth,' Naomi said, her face tense, like a gunslinger's in a duel. 'That package had the same printed label the beer mat had. Well? Didn't it?'

Karl tried laughing it off. 'Your imagination's running wild.'

'I'm within an inch of slapping that silly grin off your face. No more games or avoidance. Who's it from, and what is it?'

'I honestly don't know who it's from, and trust me, you don't want to know what it is.'

'Really?' Naomi reached over. Snatched the sleeve from Karl's hand. Held it to the light. 'What is it?'

'I hate repeating myself, but you *really* don't want to know.'

'I also hate repeating myself. What is it?'

'Don't say you weren't warned.'

'Don't worry, I won't.'

'It's a double-headed mermaid.'

Naomi turned to glare at Karl. 'A drawing of some sort?'

'A tattoo.'

'A tattoo? Like a stick-on transfer?'

'A bit more elaborate than that, I'm afraid. It's a real tattoo.'

'Real? What's that supposed to mean?'

'I believe that at one time it belonged to our friend, Graham Butler. His left forearm, if my memory serves me correctly. Someone has peeled it from his skin. That's caked blood holding it together.'

Naomi immediately dropped the sleeve. Face paled. Looked on the verge of puking.

Karl grabbed her by the elbow. 'Come on. Bathroom this way. The next time I tell you to trust me, *trust* me.'

Chapter Twenty-Nine

I watched a snail crawl along the edge of a straight razor. That's my dream; that's my nightmare. Crawling, slithering, along the edge of a straight razor…and surviving.

Colonel Walter E Kurtz, *Apocalypse Now*

Despite having listened to what sounded like the van moving off into the distance, Tara was still filled with doubt and caution. Scarman could simply have been moving the van to another part of the surrounding forest, and could now be walking back to the house, unnoticed, unheard. For all she knew, he could be down there, sitting, waiting in the dark. A trap set, and her the little mouse walking straight into it.

The winding staircase was endless. Every few steps, she stopped to listen, wishing she had remembered to take the cutthroat razor. At least she would have something to defend herself, if he grabbed her. Slice his fucking fingers right off.

Reaching the bottom of the staircase, she stood unmoving, as if trapped in icy paralysis. Her legs refused to budge, in mutiny against commands and natural instinct. Was her brain kicking into survival mode, trying to tell her something, warning her of the danger lurking right there in front of her?

She crept over to the large oak door. The three bolts were pulled back – Scarman had left, and locked the door from outside. Once, a week ago, when she thought he had fallen asleep in one of the rooms, she had sneaked down and tried the door. It wasn't locked with a key, but the three bolts had rendered it unmovable. She could manage the bottom and middle bolts, but frustratingly couldn't reach the third bolt, at the very top of the door. She almost burst into tears, being so close and yet so far.

Crouching down, she took the rest of the journey crocodile-style on knees and elbows, listening, hoping. She crawled over a group of piss-and-shit-stained mattresses, probably left behind by squatters and local drunks using the place as a booze den. A cold breeze played in the deserted hallway. It breathed along her skin, like a diseased sigh from the dying. She shivered.

In her peripheral, the rooms started coming into view. Edging to the side of the first door, she held her breath before peeping in, eyes scanning full circle. Nothing. The next four rooms followed suit. But, to her surprise, the third door on the left, the one that was reliably locked every time she had ventured downstairs, was wide open.

Something wasn't right. Directly across from the mystery room, the kitchen waited, tormenting her with its possibilities. She sniffed like a wild animal, hoping to detect something in the soulless dark, some source of food, anything to fill her aching insides.Easing down on her belly, skin tingling with nerves, she began snaking along the bare wooden floor. Thorn-like splinters bit into her bare skin, but she ignored the pain, slithering onwards into the kitchen.

In the far corner, a waste bucket. Scurrying over like a little mouse, she pulled the contents out of the bucket. *Hallelujah!* Bread. Damp and mouldy. Speckled a nasty metallic blue. It looked terrible, but to Tara, it was beautiful. Next, she discovered something meaty and slimy, held together with ugly, grey glutinous matter.

Removing a page from the middle of a pile of old newspapers in one corner, she rolled the mishmash of decayed food inside it, shoving the package up her filth-stained sweater.

Encouraged, she stood and began searching the cupboards, despite the voice pleading in her head to *get out now, before he comes back*. A squashed box of aged OXO cubes sat smiling at her from a door-less cupboard curtained with spider webs.

Tara slid her hand in, careful not to break too much of the webbing lest it leave a clue for him. Retrieved the box. Opened it. Four squashed cubes! She could almost taste the beefy tang in her mouth. She removed all the cubes. Thought better of it. Took two. Returned box to resting place.

About to tiptoe away, she stopped dead. Felt eyes tunnelling between her shoulder blades. Barely able to control her breathing, she slowly turned, expecting a huge and smirking Scarman to be standing behind her.

Nothing. Just the stagnant gloom, staring out at her from the room opposite, and – there, in the darkness! Movement. Something white and flickering. Eyes? A face, masked in shadow?

'What the…?'

It wasn't Scarman. Just a man. Strapped to a chair. Naked body, pale as wet putty. Eyes filled with madness and pain. The man's entire skin seemed ripped and shredded, covered in drying and gelling blood, pooling in the hollow of his belly's hairy button and beyond. His nipples were missing, and a great chunk of flesh had been sliced from his forearm, leaving a raw imprint with blood still leaking badly from it.

The wooden floor beneath the chair was stained a dirty red and brown, like a child's crayon drawing. Newspaper pages were pasted haphazardly on every wall, bringing the room to demented, claustrophic life. A madness of ink and blood.

'Hmmmg hmmmg…hmmmg…hmmmggggggggggg!'

The man was mumbling incoherently in muffled urgency, the tape secured to his mouth preventing the sound getting out. Like a ventriloquist's dummy in reverse.

Tara approached and stared at him, fascinated. A small, devilish smile spread across her angelic face, transforming her features into an unknown wickedness; a little imp bastardised from Satan's ballbag.

The man began shaking the chair violently, all the while mumbling his foreign, panic-stricken sounds.

'Stop with that shit!' Tara commanded.

Ignoring her, he continued shaking the chair, in a violence-gathering momentum.

'Stop it!' Frantically, Tara began searching everywhere for some sort of weapon. She soon found what she needed. A blood-stained surgical blade rested on a metal table, along with other strange, contorted cutting instruments, like medieval torture utensils. She grabbed the blade. Tipped its apex firmly under the man's chin.

'If you don't stop shaking the chair, right now, I'll fucking kill you.' Her voice was calm. Her eyes wild.

The man slowly nodded, mumbling a muffled response before halting all movement.

'I'm going to take the tape from your mouth, but I swear, you try anything, or shout, I'll plunge this blade into your throat. There's nothing I love more than blades. They've always made me powerful and dangerous. You got that?'

The man nodded, eyes showing relief, despite the threat.

With a snap, Tara pulled the tape halfway off, while keeping the blade secured beneath the man's throat.

'*Fuckkkkkkkkkkkkkkkkkkkkkkkkkkk!*' He hissed under his breath, sucking greedily on the stale air.

'Who are you?'

'My...name's...Graham Butler. Cut...cut me free...you...you've got to get...an ambulance. I've...I've lost...lots of blood...need help...'

'Why has Scarman tied you up?'

'If you're talking...talking about the maniac who tortured me, he's...he's been holding me for ransom. Did he kidnap you as well, love?'

'I'm *not* your love. Don't call me that.'

'Sorry, just thought I should know the name of the young girl who's saved my life. I'm going to make you very rich and–'

'Why would Scarman kidnap you? He's only interested in fucking little girls.'

'I've...I've already told you, he's...he's looking for money. Holding me for...ransom. I'm...a wealthy businessman.'

'Not a murdering gangster?'

'Of course not! What...whatever gave you that impression?'

'Those newspapers behind you, stuck on the wall. They say you're a well-known gangster, that you've killed innocent people.'

Butler forced a dry, painful laugh. 'Newspapers make up that...that sort of thing all the time. Just get me out...get me out of this chair before the sadistic bastard comes back. I'll... I'll take you with me.'

'You can't take me anywhere. He locks the door from outside. I've tried to open it before. It's no use.'

'My strength'll open it. You...can see the way I'm built. I'm like a bull.'

'A bull? From here, you look like a lamb, waiting to be slaughtered.'

For a split second, a look of icy glazed malevolence skated across Butler's eyes, then it melted just as quickly.

'Just get me out of this, and I'll prove to you just how strong I am.'

'I can't do that.'

Butler looked stunned. 'What…what are you on about? Can't you see what he's done to me, what he intends to do? And what about you? The bastard has done things to you, right? Probably worse than what he's done to me. Together we can escape this hellhole and–'

Tara slapped the tape back over Butler's mouth. He started shaking his head and rocking the chair aggressively, his muffled voice choking on itself.

'I trust you as much as I trust Scarman. You're all the same, all men, all monsters, all snakes. You'll say anything to get what you want.' She brought the blade away from his throat. 'I can't let you be breathing when he comes back. You'll tell him my secret. You'll tell him I was down here, searching for food. You'll tell him, so that you'll survive, you'll breathe for a little longer.'

The blade touched the raw area on Butler's arm where his mermaid tattoo was once proudly displayed. Tara eased the blade in deep, twisting and twisting, watching as the bloodletting was renewed, brighter, thicker, flowing fluently downstream without hindrance.

Butler's eyes bulged with terror and pain. He wrestled

wildly with the leather straps, twisting and turning, jerking frantically like a crazed cartoon character straddling an electric chair charged with death volts. The veins mapping his entire body started swelling. They looked on the brink of bursting, spewing all over the scene.

'Come on, come on. Get it over with. Let it go,' Tara whispered into his ear like a priest in a confessional, wishing death would come quickly for the dying, not out of compassion, but necessity. Her attention kept alternating between Butler and the door, her ears listening for the dreaded droning of the van's engine.

Butler's skin slowly paled, and then yellowed, before ultimately returning to the original pasty colour of his pre-tanning-salon days. His throat swelled like a toad in heat and then, just as quickly, deflated like a newly pricked balloon.

Almost thirty long minutes later, on the threshold of death, he urinated tea-coloured piss, and then shit himself, the bowel movement the last movement he would ever make again in his beastly, brutal bastard life, ending his nightmarish quest to conquer bloody Belfast.

Tara forced his eyelids open with her thumbs. Checked that her work was complete. The eyes stared aimlessly at the floor, as if they had spotted something soulless crawling along the filthy ground, trying to escape.

She wiped the blade on Butler's skin, then placed the lethal messenger back exactly where she had found it.

'Tara!' Relief mixed with fear animated Dorothy's face as Tara appeared out of nowhere, slipping back into the room. The bloodspot on Dorothy's neck had dried into a freckle-design. Dorothy's hand went instinctively to the tiny wound. 'I…I asked my guardian angel to watch over you.'

'Stop talking shite. Here, put this over beside the mattress while I get the bolt back in its place.' Tara handed Dorothy the package of waste food, along with the two OXO cubes.

Dorothy did as she was told. Despite the reek coming from the package, she thought it best not to complain or show her disgust.

'You were gone so long. What kept you?'

Tara glared at Dorothy. A killing look. 'It wasn't as if I had gone to Tesco, was it?'

'I…I didn't mean it that way. I just thought…something bad had happened to – you're covered in blood!'

'Huh…?'

'It's all over your jeans. Look.'

Tara stared at Butler's blood-splatter, covering most of her lower body.

'Are you hurt, Tara? What happened?'

'It's…it's nothing.'

'But all that blood and–'

'I said it's nothing! Can't you learn to listen!'

'Okay…I'm just glad you're not hurt.'

'I had my period. That's all. Don't talk any more about it.'

Tara sat down at the mattress and unwrapped the paper. The stench was even more pronounced. She offered the package to Dorothy.

'Want some?'

Dorothy felt her stomach wobble. She wanted to puke.

'No…thank you…'

'Suit yourself.' Tara shrugged her shoulders. Grounded the OXO cubes into the unholy mess. She began to feast on the devil's banquet, both hands shovelling the slop into her eager mouth in blasé pleasure.

Dorothy watched, disgusted yet fascinated. The slimy substance was sticking to Tara's face, to her lips and chin. Her eyes were crazed. She looked like a wild animal, gorging on a kill.

Tara continued gobbling the gory mess, only stopping when a photo in the newspaper-wrapping caught her eye. She uncurled the stained page of the newspaper, careful not to tear it. It was a photo of Dorothy, sitting on a sofa with a man, a woman and a littler girl the spitting image of Dorothy, only younger. The headline said: *Tragedy Of Entire Family Killed In House Fire*.

'Tara? What's wrong?'

'What…?'

'You look as if you've seen a ghost.'

Tara looked over at Dorothy. Then back to the headline.

Then back to Dorothy. She set the food down. Wiped her mouth. Tore up the newspaper.

'Come over here.'

Dorothy's stomach did a trapdoor movement of trepidation.

'But…what…what'd I do, Tara?' Dorothy knelt beside the other girl. 'I…I didn't mean to–'

Unexpectedly, Tara wrapped her arms around Dorothy, hugging her tightly.

Dorothy nervously returned the hug, then squeezed with delight at the first true touch of kindness shown to her since her arrival in this nightmarish place.

'I'm sorry for hurting you, Dorothy. Really sorry. For all the mean things I've said and done.'

'That's…that's okay, Tara. Don't worry about it. It's okay.' A smile of relief appeared on Dorothy's face as she hugged Tara even tighter.

'We're both going to be okay. You'll see. I'm going to get us out of this. Do you hear me?'

'Yes, Tara. I hear you. I hear you!'

Tears began flowing down both their faces. Both for different reasons.

Chapter Thirty

We're eyeball to eyeball, and I think the other fellow just blinked.
Dean Rusk, *Cuban Missile Crisis*

It was nearing midnight when Karl eventually called the police, but not before his card-playing lawyer friend Henry McGovern had turned up, listening to the grisly details and offering advice. Naomi sat to the right of Karl, face still pale.

When they arrived, detectives Chambers and McCormack were brought into the office and given seats. McCormack sat, studying the tattoo, absorbed by the ghastly slice of inky flesh.

Chambers nodded to Naomi.

'How are you feeling, Ms Kilpatrick?'

'Fine,' Naomi replied, her voice indicating anything but. 'I hope this isn't going to take all night? I've a splitting headache.'

'Sorry to hear that,' said Chambers, offering a sympathetic smile. 'We shouldn't be too long.'

Karl stared over at Chambers. 'I've a splitting headache also. You didn't ask how I was feeling.'

Chambers' neck reddened slightly. The smile disappeared from his face. He took the plastic container from McCormack, and held it towards Karl.

'How can you be so certain that this is Graham Butler's skin?'

'I don't want to go into particulars, but you have my word on it.'

McCormack made a mocking sound with his throat. '*Your* word?'

'That's right. My word. Don't forget, I could easily have thrown that piece of evidence in the bin. No-one would have been any the wiser.'

The corner of McCormack's upper lip curled with contempt. 'You called it in because you were afraid that down the line, word would eventually get out that you had destroyed evidence. Self-preservation. That's you in a nutshell. You're up to your neck in something. I can smell it.'

McGovern quickly stood up. 'If your associate can't restrain his thuggish attitude, Detective Chambers, then I'm afraid I'll have no alternative but to advise both of my clients to end this meeting. As Mister Kane has rightly said, he could easily have thrown the item in the bin and no-one would have been any the wiser.'

'You're right, Mister McGovern. We're very grateful to Mister Kane for calling us, and helping us with our enquiries. And Miss Kilpatrick.'

'Thank you.' McGovern nodded to Chambers, and slowly sat back down.

'And you've no idea who sent it to you, and why, Mister Kane?' Chambers continued.

'None whatsoever. I can hazard a guess and say I don't think it was Graham Butler.'

'Those kind of flippant remarks don't help. You realise we're going to have to take your fingerprints, so that we can eliminate them from any we may find on the package?'

In a flash, McGovern held up his hand. 'That won't be happening, Detective. Unless you have a court order, of course?'

'No, we don't have a court order at the moment, Mister McGovern. I can understand you trying to safeguard your clients' interests, but all it's doing is wasting valuable time, when we could be out looking for the abductor or abductors of Mister Butler.'

Karl false laughed. 'And I'm supposed to trust you that my fingerprints won't conveniently appear somewhere else, say a gun or a bloody knife?'

'I can give you assurances that—'

'You can't give me anything, particularly *assurances,* if past experience with the neurotic behaviour of your boss, Wilson, is anything to go by.'

'You're hindering police work, Kane!' McCormack slapped his hand loudly on the table. 'I wonder the hell why?'

'You really need to keep attending those anger-management classes, McCormack. Your face looks like it's ready to melt.'

McGovern looked at his watch, before addressing the gathering. 'Gentlemen, I think we should call it a night. As you can appreciate, this has been a very distressful experience for my client, and also for Miss Kilpatrick. Both deserve a good night's sleep.'

Chambers nodded and stood. McCormack stared over at Karl, before reluctantly standing also.

'If you can think of anything else to help us, it would be very much appreciated, Mister Kane,' Chambers said, eye-levelling Karl.

'Of course. You'll be the first to know,' Karl said, not too convincingly, but not dropping his eyes.

Chambers seemed on the verge of saying something, but instead merely blinked, then turned and left. McCormack stalled for a few seconds, before leaving also.

As soon as the detectives exited, Karl walked McGovern to the door, thanking him.

'Don't talk to the police unless I'm present, Karl,' advised McGovern. 'And for God's sake, watch yourself. Please tell Naomi the same.'

'Thanks again, Henry, for getting here so soon.'

'I can't have anything happening to you, with all the money you owe me,' McGovern smiled.

Karl watched McGovern drive away before going back inside. Naomi had left, gone upstairs. Karl extinguished all the lights, and followed suit. Naomi was sitting on the sofa in the living room.

'Want a nightcap before we hit the sack, Naomi?'

'How much trouble are you in?'

'Trouble? None. Why're you asking?'

'You didn't mention to the police that the tattoo and beer mat came from the same person.'

'Who's the private investigator here?'

'Or about the phone call earlier tonight.'

Karl looked at her for a very long time before answering.

'You want to know about the beer mat, and everything else that goes along with it? Want to know my darkest secrets? Think you're strong enough to listen to my nightmares?'

'What's got into you, talking like that? All I want is for you to–'

'No. None of that old shite about only being concerned about me. You don't get to pick or choose, Naomi. Not this time, you don't. You're asking for the darkness of the genie to be released from its bottle? Okay, but just remember: you *don't* get to put the genie back in the bottle, once it's been released.'

Chapter Thirty-One

I can hear you whisperin' children, so I know you're down there.
I can feel myself gettin' awful mad. I'm out of patience children.
I'm coming to find you now.
Reverend Harry Powell, *The Night of the Hunter*

Tara debated with herself about whether to tell Dorothy
the dreadful news of what had happened to her family.

She remembered herself as a kid – not that she wasn't a kid
still, but an awful lot had changed in her mind – lonely, no
family, no friends. Just strangers. Brutal strangers, beating and
sexually abusing her. She remembered learning to fight dirty,
because life *was* dirty. The only thing the meek inherited was
pain and suffering, not the Earth as slimy old Pastor Kilkee
murmured in her ear every night at Blackmore, while forcing
his sharp, bony fingers up her thighs.

She thought about how they had thrown her into that
padded cell, straightjacket corseting her entire body; about
the sharpened knitting needles she had rammed into the Pastor's eyeballs, forcing the shafts all the way into his brain. She
had survived. She would survive this also, because she knew
how to fight dirty; she knew not to beg for help.

Dorothy was resting on her back. Eyes closed tightly. Lips barely moving, whispering to herself. She seemed in some sort of trance.

'Have you lost the plot, talking to yourself?'

'I'm not talking to myself. I'm…I'm just saying my prayers, asking God to help get us out of here.'

'I've already told you, we will get out of here. But we'll have to do it ourselves. No-one else – including turn-a-blind-eye God – is going to help.'

'My mum and dad'll help. They won't give up until they find me. Then you can come and live with us, Tara. Our wee Cindy would love you. She's a pain in the arse, but she's funny and cute. She's always laughing.'

'Don't be…don't be getting your hopes up too much…'

'Why? Don't you want to come and live with–?'

'*Shhhhhhhhhhhhhhhh!*'

The sound of an engine could be heard chugging to a stop.

'What is it, Tara?'

'*He's back.*'

Dorothy began hyperventilating, sucking on the air as if having an asthma attack.

'Will…will he know you…were downstairs? What will… what will he do to us, Tara, if he…if he finds out?'

Scarman emerged from the van. Walked casually to the front door of the house, carrying a couple of decoys: supermarket bags filled with rags and garbage, lest some nosey neighbour spot him, watching his comings and goings. One has to be careful in such isolated areas. Bored people with too much time on their hands quickly learn to become curtain-twitching experts.

He closed the front door behind him, dropping the decoys where he stood. About to walk down the hallway, he hesitated. His body stiffened, nostrils flaring slightly. He sniffed. Something. What? A smell interrupting the other smells, dominating the air.

He prowled down the hallway, sniffing like a bloodhound on a trail. Different smells began webbing inside his nasal cavities: dust, grease, sourness. Blood.

He focused on the blood. Fresh. Damp. From the back of his waistband, he extracted a knife, moving silently on down the hallway, a ghost of a man preparing to meet a ghost of something else, its sell-by-date expired.

He edged his head against the doorframe. A splinter of the room came into view. Butler. Slumped over his bondage, as if cleaved in half.

Scarman's eyes darted from corner to corner. He waited a few seconds before stepping inside. He didn't need to touch the body to see that Butler was gone. A bluish hue glazed the skin. His bottom lip hung ghoulishly from the dangling duct tape.

Butler had managed to bite his way through the tape, as well as his lip. The plump lip looked like a bloody garden slug captured on flypaper.

Had the gangster deliberately gnawed his own lip off, so as to die, no longer able to endure what he had forced others to endure? He didn't think Butler was suicidally inclined. Surely Butler would have done anything to stay alive, to save his own skin?

A wry smile appeared on Scarman's face at the unintended pun. Still, who knows what breaks one man but makes another?

Scarman knelt on one knee. Began examining the body, paying particular attention to the skin on the forearm he had sliced off and sent to Kane. Blood bumps lined the border of missing skin. Older skin had curled back, exposing growth killed in its genesis.

He pressed down on one of the bumps. It was spongy, blood trapped beneath its tiny dome. The blood was discoloured. Two shades. One on top of the other.

These were fresh cuts. But how?

He glanced over at the table where the surgical blades rested. Looked at the blade he had used earlier. Stood, then walked over to the table. Lifted the blade by the end of its handle. Held it close to his eyes and examined it, before leaving the room. He headed back along the hallway, the blade dangling at his side.

At the bottom of the winding staircase, Scarman stopped, blade raised in preparation. He peered directly above him, in the direction of the girls' room. He continued staring, trance-like, for the longest time, until startled by a loud banging on the front door.

Upstairs, Tara was peeping out the small hole she had managed to make beneath the window frame.

'*There's someone down there, at the front door!*' she whispered.

'*Who is it, Tara? Can you see?*' said Dorothy, controlled excitement in her voice.

Tara squeezed her eye tighter against the hole. '*It's…it's a man. He's got a gun. A big fucking gun!*'

'It must be the police! They've come to rescue us! Shout out to them. Hurry!'

Scarman stood, debating with himself, his grip tightening on the blade.

More knocking. Insistent. It seemed to echo everywhere in the hallway, like a wooded creature of flight let loose, banging off the walls.

He walked silently to the front door. Bent his sight to the peephole, just as Tara was doing directly above him.

It was a man, cradling a menacing-looking weapon in his arms. He had a ruddy, weatherbeaten face and shrewd, determined eyes. By his attire, he did not appear to be a cop – at least not a city cop – and definitely not in uniform. Could be the local cop, off-duty, acquainting himself with people newly moved into the area.

'Hello? Anyone home?' said the man, staring directly into the peephole and Scarman's eye.

Scarman calculated the pros and cons of opening the door. Sit it out, and wait for him to depart, leaving open the distinct possibility of his return? Take him by surprise, pull him into the house, slit his throat? Of course, that would create its own problems, if he had family and they started wondering where he was. Miscalculations and rushed moves were the root of all perfect plans laid to waste.

He opted for the only realistic option available. Opened the front door.

'Yes?' Scarman kept his right hand behind his back, the blade ready to go to war.

'Apologies for the shotgun. Just in case I run into a fox,' Francis Duffy said, patting the shotgun and smiling.

'What is it you want?'

'I'm really sorry for bothering you. I'm Francis Duffy, your next-door neighbour, so to speak.' Francis offered a handshake. Scarman ignored it. 'I own the farm, a couple of minutes down the road.'

Chapter Thirty-One

'And?'

'Er, yes, just letting you know, my sheep have a terrible tendency to wander away at all times of night. They end up in all sorts of places. If they happen to be seen nibbling your front lawn, I'll pay for any damage they cause.'

'This is private property. I didn't send out any invites to you or your sheep. Don't trespass again.'

Scarman closed the door, and resumed his watching position at the peephole.

Francis remained, looking at the door, staring at the peephole. It was almost a minute later before he made his way down the pathway and out through the gates.

After Francis had left, Scarman remained standing there for a long time. He couldn't afford confrontation at this moment. Too many long years had gone into preparation and planning to see it ruined by some straw-sucking, sheep-shagging oaf.

Farmers knew the lay of the land like the muck on their wellies. Re-arrangements of features upsetting the landscape didn't go unobserved by them. A broken twig, blades of grass trampled on, bushes reshaped by pushing bodies, all made farmers naturally cagey and suspicious. They were constantly vigilant.

This farmer posed a problem. The question was: how big a problem?

Chapter Thirty-Two

I measure out my time in blue pills,
hoping to chase the blues away.

Karl Kane

Karl and Naomi sat on the bed, facing the dressing table near the far window. With the lights turned off in the room, the streetlamp directly facing the window filled the room in a weary greyness.

Karl reflectively watched his own reflection in the dullness of the table's mirror. He looked wasted and lost, like a book with missing pages, or a man for whom time had finally run out. A glass of brandy rested tantalisingly on the small bedroom table, but he refused to touch it. He would do this without the assistance of Mister Hennessy.

Naomi, wrapped in a nightgown, was looking concerned. A terrible tension was stalking the room, like a hand grenade with the pin about to be pulled.

'Why don't we get into bed, Karl? You'll be a lot more comfortable.'

'Thinking of sex again, Miss Kilpatrick?' Karl false-smiled. It made him look even older than he felt, right at this moment in life. 'Remember after we first met, and were getting to know each other a bit better?'

'Haemorrhoids, love of brandy, divorced, lousy at gambling, great at sex…?'

'No, that was you. I'm talking about me!' said Karl, smiling.

They both laughed. A nervous laugh. Unnatural.

'I confided in you about my mother being attacked and raped, and then murdered, by Walter Arnold, when I was nine?'

'Yes, and I know how hard is was for you to discuss it.' Naomi squeezed Karl's hand reassuringly. 'Don't bring up the past, Karl. You know it's not good for you.'

'But the past is killing me, destroying the present. That's why I need to lance it from my system, once and for all. I need to put myself back in the driving seat, instead of just being a hijacked passenger. Remember how I told you that Arnold left me for dead after stabbing me multiple times?'

Naomi shuddered. 'Yes.'

'What I *never* told you was that he…he…' Karl's voice trailed off. He inhaled a large gulp of air, and then very slowly exhaled. 'He…raped me…'

Naomi looked stunned. Her mouth opened, but no words came out. Her eyes registered shock and horror. She tried to regain her composure, but failed.

'Karl…oh my Karl…' She wrapped her arms protectively around his neck and shoulders. Her eyes began to fill with tears. 'My poor Karl…'

'Don't start with the crying. This is hard enough for me. And if you continue squeezing my neck, you're going to break it,' Karl said, hugging Naomi reassuringly before easing her grip on his neck.

Naomi wiped away her tears, but more followed. 'Why… why didn't you tell me this before? Didn't you trust me?'

'I've never told *anyone*; not even Lynne when I was married to her. Not my father. You're the first.'

'But why did you wait this long, keep it all bottled up inside of you?'

'Perhaps it was just a macho thing; that men can't be raped. The stigma of it, and the shame.'

'Shame? But this…this had nothing to do with you. You were the victim, a child.'

'I know that. That's logic speaking, but the reality is a different animal entirely. I've always felt ashamed about it, as if I somehow contributed to the rape. Even in the psychotherapy sessions I was given after my mother's murder, I never once mentioned the rape. I was afraid of how the psychotherapist would react to me. I don't want sympathy or pity, just understanding of the way I behave sometimes. Joking and laughing about things I shouldn't. Of things I have done…'

'Things? What things?'

He looked away, unable to meet her gaze. 'Terrible things…'

Naomi reached over, tenderly clasping his head in both her hands.

'Look at me, Karl. *Look* at me.'

Slowly, his eyes rested on hers. He wanted to dissolve away into them, wanted them to erase all the bad things. The nightmares. The perpetual darkness.

'You, Karl Kane, are the best thing to *ever* happen to me. Full stop. You're the kindest, the most loving, the most bighearted man I know. Do you understand that? Do you *understand* how much I love–'

'I killed two young girls…children…'

Naomi's face turned to the colour of damp snow.

'What…? What are you talking about, Karl? Why would you say something so horrible?'

'Ann Mullin and Leona Fredrick. Both aged eight. Raped, then murdered.'

'But…Arnold committed those horrible crimes, not you.'

'I could've prevented him. That makes me equally guilty.'

'No. That's ridiculous. You can't think that way.'

'Is it? For years, I lived with nothing but revenge on my mind. Revenge, to kill Arnold for what he did to Mum, to me. Then, one Good Friday night, many years later, I had the opportunity. I'd been watching his habits and behaviours for over a year, following him all around Belfast. I knew that every second or third Friday he went to his favourite restaurant, Fiddler's Green–'

'Fiddler's Green…? The beer mat?'

'That's right. I was armed with the holy trinity of retribution: gun, determination and justification.'

Outside the apartment, a heavy rain began to assault the window, as though a million crows on the verge of starvation had found victuals scattered in the wilderness of God's open palm.

Karl listened to the rain intently, almost hypnotised. He shuddered.

'It was raining that night, also, just like this…'

He reached and lifted the brandy glass to his lips. This time, he surrendered, filled his mouth with the agreeable liquid. Let it sea against his parched tongue, as if it could exorcise the bad taste of memory. Swallowed what his mouth held. Set the glass back down.

'I followed Arnold when he came out of Fiddler's Green. I followed him along the Antrim Road. Pitch-black night, as dark as the devil's heart. Little or no traffic, human or metal. I came within arm's length of him when he suddenly stopped dead-weight in his tracks.'

'Did…did he see you?' Naomi had been hanging on to every word, like a butcher's hook embedded into bloody meat. Tense, she had barely moved a muscle, trapped in Karl's dark, claustrophobic world of violence and retribution.

'He'd stopped to take a piss. I walked closer; so close I could smell the stench of that piss, the booze seeping through his filthy pores, his Old Spice aftershave, the greasy Brylcreem stuck to his hair.'

'You don't have to continue, Karl. It's okay.'

'I aimed the gun at the back of his head, thinking of the evil he had perpetrated, on Mum, on me. I tried to say his name, make him turn around, face me. But my tongue refused to move. I squeezed on the trigger, gritted my teeth, waited for the explosion of brain and skull, but…I couldn't do it. I had the bastard in my sights, and I couldn't fucking do it.'

Karl's hands were trembling with anger. Knuckles white, almost popping from their fleshy enclosure.

'Easy…easy, love,' Naomi whispered. *'You're better than Arnold. That's why you couldn't do it.'*

'Within forty-eight hours, he had abducted little Ann and Leona, raped and murdered them in the most brutal fashion. They were out egg-painting on Easter Sunday. I could have saved them, but I was a coward.'

'That's guilt talking, Karl. You can't change the past. Arnold murdered Ann and Leona. Not you. He was given life imprisonment for that.'

'The law deemed him insane when he murdered my mother. He was put away for five years in a mental institute. *Five bloody years!* Can you believe that? Had he been given life at the time, he wouldn't have been out on the streets, able to murder those two kids, twenty years later.'

'The whole thing was a travesty of justice, Karl. Nothing can change that, no matter how much you persecute yourself.'

'Justice? Justice had nothing to do with it. Money was the principle factor. Arnold came from one of the wealthiest families in Belfast, and to this day, I believe the so-called judge – that fucker William Pickering – had his pockets filled with blood money by Arnold's parents for a shorter sentence.'

Naomi held him, rocking her tired and defeated partner – *her man* – gently, whispering soft and calming things into his ear meant for him and no other. He closed his eyes, allowing his body to move with her gentle sways. She hummed a song, something barely audible and arcane. Something magic. Something only women know the meaning to, and hold its trust in their bosoms.

He couldn't remember when exactly he had fallen asleep, but he did, in her arms.

Chapter Thirty-Three

The dumber people think you are, the more surprised they're
going to be when you kill them.
William Clayton (aka Billy the Kid)

Despite the fierce storm raging unabated, Scarman had taken to a narrow vein of backroads and unventured pathways, all overgrown with wild, thorny bushes and weeds the size of menacing triffids. The rain fell like freezing ball bearings, increasing the weight of the darkness. The weather suited his purposes well.

This nighttime world he traversed seemed void of all moving and breathing things, long abandoned by gods and good people. To Scarman, though, it was faultless. It filled him with an inexpressible sensation so wondrously sweet he felt a renewed understanding of his own destiny and footprint in life.

After five minutes of walking, slowed and hindered constantly by the undergrowth, he came to the lone and lonely farmhouse. It waited there for him like a resigned silhouette clipped from funereal paper. The sight made him grin his wolf's grin. He was the aggrieved party, the police, the prosecution, the expert witness, the judge, the jailor, the executioner, the undertaker. He was the hunter.

The back of the house was blocked by congregations of rusting machinery, along with rotten timber felled eons ago by the eager axe and wiry muscles of promise and enthusiasm. Now, all life was gone; relegated to an era long departed and long forgotten. Neglect had finally been crowned prince and conqueror.

Scarman approached the side of the house, populated by two rusted tractors and moss-covered equine items, soldiered side-by-side with an army of worthless tools, as ancient as any-thing utilised by Noah in his wooded chandlery as he waited for the great rains of judgement to burst forth.

Edging himself up to an ageing, naked window, he peered where his eyes guided. The window belonged to a one-time bedroom, now chock-a-block with floor-to-ceiling clutter. Paper mainly. Reams of books towered in skyline formation. Magazines carpeted the floor. Yellowing newspapers suffocated ancient and rickety-looking furniture.Beyond that bedroom, the hallway; beyond the hallway, the living room, a sequence of shapes and shade. In the living room, shadows fashioned from a log-fed fire danced in crazed movements.

Rain was sloshing against the windowpane, interrupting his voyeurism. Still, he was able to catch a measured view of the living room, and a pair of legs stretched out. The legs were almost hugging the blazing fire. A shotgun rested not too far from the legs, like a faithful hound awaiting its master's deadly command.

He slid back down to the ground. The wetted muck was becoming swampier. Less traction accorded for his intended deeds.

Deadly, dark deeds.

The rain continued its unpitying torrent. Drowning him. He almost missed the basement door, camouflaged as it was in dung and wet leaves.

Looking all about, he schemed and weighed options, purchasing a rusted pipe, flattened and eroded by time and the elements. With this, he began to scrape away leaves and roots and dung. It was human dung. Not animal. He uprooted the dung, digging under it. Its belly glistened like something malevolent from a cursed swampland. The slimy mess clung to the pipe like a crazed dog in lockjaw. The stench was overpowering. Male in all its ugliness. Not like the young girls'. No, not like theirs at all.

He pictured the ancient farmer eating all those filthy turnips, sprouts and spuds, shovelling them down his toothless mouth before going to the shitter, sitting down and releasing his load like an animal giving birth. He hated the farmer even more now, quickly horseshoeing the bar's metal lip between gaps in the wooden shutters and bordering cement.

His brute force laid siege to the primitive doors, until they eventually shuddered, then splintered into surrender.

He pulled back the remains. Darkness beckoned. As he was about to enter, something bit him in the leg.

King stood, snarling, face pulled back over its skull, red eyes wide, teeth bared and prepared for battle.

'Easy boy…' Scarman hissed, turning carefully, hoping not to spook the dog into attacking him. He clamped the rusted pipe in his fist, and readied it.

King leapt forward, snapping at him. He threw a wild swing. The pipe hit King on the side of the head. King yelped, but came right back again, knocking the pipe from Scarman's hand and sinking its curved teeth into the leg of his trousers. A tug-of-war ensued. Scarman pulled on the trouser leg, struggling to free it from the dog's grip. King dug its heels in, its head tearing from side to side in a sawing motion.

'Bastard!' This time Scarman lashed out, landing a solid kick to King's nose.

The creature whimpered loudly, then turned and ran as fast as its feet could carry it.

Shaken, Scarman entered the basement, and was immediately swallowed up.

In front of the comfort of his fire, Francis reflected on Karl's visit two days ago. Perhaps he shouldn't have proffered the information about Cornelius and Martha Johnson having an affair? He had clearly seen the shock in Karl's eyes, and also the hurt. It was the last thing he had ever wanted to do, to hurt the lad.

'Damn it! You're like an old wine vessel, bursting at the seams.' He couldn't stop admonishing himself. 'Can't keep anything in. You damn fool. If Nora still lived, you'd have had a verbal lashing from her.'

The thought of his beloved wife instantly made him feel terribly alone and melancholy. He craned a log from a side-basket, and unceremoniously dropped it into the grate. Sparks spat out at him, landing on his liver spots and withered hands. He watched the sparks die on his skin. If they caused pain, he did not submit to it, nor offer deposition.

Standing up from the large, threadbare armchair, he removed Karl's card from the top of the old working table. He tried the phone again. The third time today. Still not working. Power lines brought down by the storm.

First thing in the morning, he'd call Karl, tell him about the new owner in the old house. Something not right about the man. Those eyes.

Francis Duffy didn't scare easily, but he had to admit to himself, the eyes *had* unnerved him. He was relieved when the man quickly closed the door in his face.

Francis put the card back on the table, and walked over to the cupboard. Removed a solitary teabag and the sugar bag. Placed the teabag in the teapot. Clicked the kettle's water into life, and went back to making himself comfortable in the armchair.

The logs sparked, hissed and spat, lighting up the room in sporadic bursts, like a miniature fireworks display. He stared into the flames' dancing tongues, licking at the trembling logs. They were hypnotic. He thought he saw Nora's face in them. She was smiling at him, calling out his name.

Francis…Francis…

That was when he noticed the shotgun had vanished.

Chapter Thirty-Four

My eyes have seen what my hand did.
Robert Lowell, *Dolphin*

The storm lasted throughout the night and into the early hours of the morning. It had little effect on Karl's usual sunny disposition.

'The noise last night,' he grumbled, sipping his early morning coffee at the kitchen table. He looked like a bear forced out of hibernation. 'Sounded like the end of the world.'

Naomi smiled, kissed him and sat down opposite, a bowl of cereal in her hands. 'I slept like a baby. I hardly heard the storm.'

'It wasn't the storm I was referring to, it was your bloody snoring.'

'I'll have you know, Karl Kane, I do *not* snore. I'm a lady.'

'Then it must have been all that farting you were doing, because some sort of thundering noise was coming from you, from under the sheets as well as—'

The front doorbell sounded. Karl and Naomi looked at each other, neither moving. A Mexican standoff.

The bell sounded again. More insistent this time.

Naomi sighed, stood to get up.

'Don't bother,' said Karl, standing. 'I'll do it, like everything else around here.'

'Keep telling yourself that. Might come true one day.'

Opening the front door, he was struck with surprise and weariness by the sight of Detective Chambers, notebook clutched in one hand.

'I'll have to move you into the spare room, if you keep showing up at my door, Chambers. What is it now?'

'Can I come in?'

'This early in the morning? Catch yourself on.'

'Okay. I'll ask the questions here. How well did you know a Francis Duffy?'

Karl's stomach clenched in trepidation.

'What's happened to Francis?'

'He was found dead at his home in the early hours of yesterday morning. A district nurse who checks in on him occasionally discovered the body.'

'Ah shit…' Karl shook his head. 'What…what happened?'

'Initial reports suggest a burglary gone wrong. Looks like a struggle between Mister Duffy and the perpetrator ended when Mister Duffy was shot in the stomach with his own legally-held shotgun.'

Karl could no longer hold back the rage. 'Fuck! For all he had, some scumbag would kill him. Bastard! And to shoot him in the stomach…'

'Was Mister Duffy related to you in any way?'

'No...not related, more a friend of the family from many years back. What makes you think it was a burglary?'

Chambers scribbled something into the notebook before addressing Karl. 'The house had been ransacked, apparently. Hard to tell what was stolen. According to the report, everything seemed to be haphazardly strewn about.'

Karl thought back to the state of the place when he had visited. It already looked like it had been ransacked.

'Do the cops have any leads? Any suspects? *Anything*?'

Chambers shook his head. 'Forensic officers are still going over the scene. It'll be some time before we hear from them.'

'Any other questions? I'm going to have to make funeral arrangements for Francis, ASAP.'

'Did Mister Duffy have any enemies that you know of?'

Karl shook his head. 'I really couldn't answer that. Up until a week ago, I hadn't seen him in years. He seemed to be living a hermit's existence, just wanting to be left alone.'

'What exactly were you doing, visiting him?'

Karl's face tightened. 'The damn answer is in your question, smartarse. Visiting. Not that it's any of your business. Anything else? I need to go.'

'If you think of anything, anything you may have...forgotten, will you contact me?'

Karl nodded. 'Now, I really need to move it.'

'Of course.'

Chambers turned to leave just as something occured to Karl.

'You haven't told me how you figured I might have a connection with Francis.'

The young detective stared at Karl, reluctance in his demeanour.

'I…I didn't want to tell you at this stage.'

'Jesus, drop the cryptic shit, Chambers. Tell me what?'

'Your business card…it was stapled to Mister Duffy's forehead.'

Chapter Thirty-Five

Of all God's creatures, there is only one that cannot be made slave of the leash. That one is the cat. If man could be crossed with the cat it would improve the man, but it would deteriorate the cat.
Mark Twain, *Notebook*, 1894

At Francis Duffy's graveside, Karl huddled under Naomi's umbrella, sheltering from the rain and biting wind. The combined power of the elements had successfully managed to drown out all other sounds, making it difficult for Karl to hear the minister's message at the lowering of the coffin.

Not that Karl paid much attention to messengers from god, but he was always fascinated by how their words could be shaped and formulated to be used for balm or bane, Hell or Heaven, salvation or ruination.

Shit! He was beginning to sound like one of those firebrand preachers, all the words in rhyme and time, congregation sweating profusely like Madam Juicy Lucy, eyeballs rolling and scolding, winking ever-knowing.

Francis' lone existence was reflected in the meagre collection of onlookers, a two-hand count, which included Karl,

Naomi, Chambers, the preacher, three gravediggers and a couple of stragglers from an earlier funeral.

Why in the hell would people want to attend the funeral of someone they didn't even know? wondered Karl, staring at the two stragglers. *Is this how they get their day in? Visiting grave-yards, regardless of the weather or random deceased? Do they have a little black book and compare coffins, a bit like train spotting. Was there an entire industry of ghouls, lurking, searching like junkies for their next fix of death?*

Nothing would surprise him any more. He had seen too much darkness in this ghastly world, to rule anything out that could be deemed *sociably acceptable*.

He looked from the stragglers to Chambers, standing with head down. When he confronted the young detective on why he was here, Chambers didn't miss a beat:

I'm on duty. Watching to see if the killer shows up. They do that sometimes.

Yes, in bloody Agatha Christie novels...

Bullshit. He was here to sneak a glance at Naomi, all dressed in black. Of that, Karl had little doubt.

Just as his thoughts were sliding into paranoia, his mobile started bleating in his coat pocket. He hated the thought of taking his gloves off in this freezing rain, just to answer it. He didn't want to hear echoing voices today. He got enough echo-ing voices in his nightmares, night after night.

'Not going to turn that off, Karl?' Naomi nudged him with

her elbow. It was a demand. Not a question. 'The minister's looking over here. You're interrupting his eulogy.'

'Well, he should be looking upwards or downwards, not over in this direction. Anyway, he didn't even know Francis. He'll hardly lose any sleep over it tonight.'

'Just turn it *off*,' Naomi said in a not-too-happy voice. 'So disrespectful.'

He let it ring, more to aggravate her than anything else. After a few more seconds, it went dead.

'Happy now?' said Karl, as Naomi visibly relaxed.

Just as he spoke, it started ringing again. Naomi glared at him. He quickly retrieved the offending device from his pocket. Glanced at the number on the screen, and then switched it off.

'Who was it?' Naomi asked.

'Shouldn't you be paying attention to the minister? So disrespectful.'

Back at the office, Karl called Tommy Naughton back.

'Tommy? Sorry, I couldn't answer your phone call earlier. I was at a funeral. No, not family, just an old neighbour. When? Now? I don't know, Tommy, I've an awful lot of work to–' Karl nodded to himself. 'Okay, Tommy. Calm down. Yes, I'll be there shortly.'

Karl clicked the phone off.

'What did Tommy want?' Naomi asked.

'A bit confusing. Thinks that god-damn creepy cat they own may have seen the intruder on the night of the fire.'

'The cat *saw* someone?'

'The cat saw someone. Don't ask me what the hell that means. I'm away to see him now, see what this is all about. Look after the fort until I get back. I shouldn't be long.'

He gave Naomi a quick kiss and then marched back outside on a fool's errand, cold, damp and miserable.

Karl, Tommy and Theresa were gathered in the living room. Theresa's eyes were puffy and red, as if she had recently been crying. She looked upset. Tiddles the cat snoozed, crescent-shaped atop the sofa, oblivious to the drama being acted out in its presence and name.

In Tommy's palm, a tiny plastic bauble nestled like a robin's egg.

'Pauline bought it for Tiddles a few months ago,' Tommy explained, his voice quivering with emotion.

A puzzled-looking Karl took the item and began scrutinising it. 'What…what exactly is it?'

'They call it "Cat-Eye". It's like a miniature spy camera for cats. Pauline saw it on one of those animal shows, about a town full of cats, and what the cats get up to at night, unknown to their owners. Pauline said it was fascinating to watch. The very next day, she went out and bought one for Tiddles.'

'Tiddles wasn't too happy at the start, mind you, having it wrapped around her neck like a millstone,' Theresa said, a sad smile on her face. 'But eventually she got used to it. We always watched it about once a week, just to see what she'd get up to on the nights she was out prowling.'

'So, that's what was on her neck when I first saw her?' Karl said, amazed. 'Isn't it remarkable what these gadget-people can do, nowadays? How everything is becoming so miniaturised?'

'We were watching it about an hour ago, and we got an awful shock at what we saw, didn't we, Tommy?' Theresa said.

'Yes, love. A real shock.' Tommy nodded in agreement.

'Put it on for Karl, will you, Tommy?'

Tommy inserted the USB stick into the computer's port, and clicked the word 'PLAY' on the screen. The video came to life:

Darkness. Then grey fuzziness. Slowly clearing. A cat's-eye view of a hidden nocturnal, purgatorial world, inhabited by posses of shadows closing in all around in a smothering claustrophia. The fish-eye lens made it seem as if the video was playing out on a spoon's curved surface. Shaky streaks of images rose up: a spider building its esoteric web, blueprint wired to its ancient brain of dried bone powder. A partial cat paw demolishing the web with one swipe. Spider impaled on a curved claw. Chewed to a bloody inkblot. Then…stillness. Cat's attention is now arrowed elsewhere. More shaky movements. Then steady again. A figure emerges from the back door of the house. Carrying something. Booty, perhaps?

'Do you see him, Karl, coming out the back door?' Theresa said.

'Stop it right there, Tommy.' Karl brought his face closer to the screen.

Tommy clicked STOP. Karl studied the image, the shadowy, androgynous figure. *Is the person actually coming out the back door of the house? Or is that an adjacent entry? Hard to tell. Could be a man. Could be a woman. Is that a nylon stocking pulled over the head to obscure identity? A devil uninvited.*

'Isn't that the creepiest thing you ever saw, Karl?' Tommy said.

'Huh? Oh…yes, Tommy…' lied Karl, having not only seen creepier things, but experienced them as well. *Bundle in arms? Hard to distinguish through the grainy quality of the nighttime recording, and the medieval attire the figure has itself wrapped in.*

'That's a man,' Theresa said, pointing at the screen. 'I've no doubt about it.'

'Could it be one of the people at the party?' Karl said.

'See down in the bottom corner? There's a time stamp on it. This was four in the morning. The party had finished long before this happened. Everyone left at the same time. This man is an intruder, and that's either our wee Cindy or

Chapter Thirty-Five

Dorothy he has in his filthy arms.'

Karl continued studying. Saying nothing. He had doubts as to gender; doubts as to what was being carried. It didn't look like a small body.

Tommy re-clicked PLAY.

The cat has halted all movement. Transfixed with total concentration in the moment of the mysterious vignette. Intruder is moving slowly away across the yard. Steps over puddle-like carcass of an animal.

'Is that a dead dog?' Karl asked.

Theresa nodded. 'Samson, the family pet. Poor thing. He was a lovely dog. He loved those girls.'

Figure suddenly stops. Starts looking about. Hesitant, scanning the yard. Stares over towards Cat-Eye, as if watching Karl's voyeurism.

The hairs on the back of Karl's neck rose and prickled. A sheen of cold sweat skimmed off his spine. He could hardly breathe. *What the fuck…?*

'That's Dorothy or Cindy! God, I know it is!' screamed Theresa.

Tommy put his arm over Theresa's shoulder, trying to reassure her. 'Easy, love. Easy…we don't know if it–'

'Don't you dare, Tommy Naughton! Don't you dare question my grandmotherly intuition,' said Theresa, pushing Tommy away. 'I don't care what you think – or *anyone*. That's one of our grandkids wrapped up in that blanket.'

Diplomatically sidestepping the potential quarrel, Karl clicked the STOP button.

'Look, we need to be watching this video together, not arguing. Afterwards, we'll share our opinions of what we saw. Okay?'

Tommy nodded. Theresa followed his example, but with obvious reluctance.

Karl clicked PLAY.

Figure slowly places bundle on ground. Now reaching for something beneath clothing. Slowly bringing up hand. A knife? Figure slowly stands. Quite crafty. Like lightning, throws knife. Madness ensues. Images bobbing up and down. Cat running. Like hell.

Hell…

'The dirty bastard,' Tommy said. 'See the way he threw that knife at Tiddles?'

Karl continued watching for over a minute, but nothing else of importance seemed to follow. He clicked STOP.

'Well, Karl? What did *you* see?' Theresa said, looking at Karl with a paradoxical mixture of despair and hope in her sad eyes.

'Can I get a copy of the film put on a disc?' Karl said to Tommy, deliberately ignoring Theresa's question.

'Not too sure how to do that, Karl,' Tommy said. 'Pauline would do all that kind of stuff.'

'No problem. I have a friend who knows everything there

is to know about computers. Just give me the original USB stick, and I'll get copies made.'

'Karl?' Theresa said. 'What did you see?'

Karl turned, looked at Theresa, and said, 'My daughter, Katie, was kidnapped, over two years ago, Theresa, so don't think for one moment I don't understand the hell you and Tommy are going through.'

'Dear lord, Karl.' Theresa put her hand to her mouth, looking completely stunned. 'I'm so sorry…did…did you get her back?'

Physically, not mentally. 'I…I got her back…eventually. So, let's not lose hope. Hope is everything. With your permission, I'll give a copy of this to the police. I know how you feel about cops, but we're going to need all the help we can get.'

'Give it to them. If they can bring Dorothy or Cindy back, I'll be eternally grateful to them.'

Karl looked away from Theresa, his eyes resting on the family portrait on the fireplace. Two young girls looked out at him. *Both* dead? One alive? Just like Theresa, his intuition was kicking in. However, his was telling him this wasn't going to end up a happy-ever-after story.

Chapter Thirty-Six

This place is dangerous. The time right deadly.
The drinks are on me, my bucko!
Mark Cardigan, *His Kind of Woman*

'Take the weight off your feet, sit down.' Karl said to Detective Chambers, standing beside his table in Debbie Does Dinners, a well-known café on Great Victoria Street in the city centre, not a kick in the arse away from the Europa hotel. It was the day after the Naughtons played Karl the Cat-Eye video.

'What's this all about, Kane? You said it was urgent. I've just come off the nightshift; I need to get home for some sleep.'

'Coffee?' Karl asked, as a young waitress approached the table.

'White,' Chambers said, reluctantly sitting down. 'Two sugars.'

'What can I get you gentlemen?' the waitress asked, smiling a tired but management-ordered smile.

'Two coffees, Mary. The usual for me. White and two sugars for my friend here. Where's Janice? Off?'

'Dying with the flu, Karl. Hasn't been in all week.'

'She must be bad. She'd work eight days a week, given the chance.'

Chambers waited until the waitress had left

'Why'd you want to meet me here, of all places?'

'Why not? This is one of my regular eating joints.'

'Lots of police officers eat here.'

'Very observant of you. And your point is?'

'Just thought…well…'

'Just thought I'd be intimidated in the presence of a load of cops who hate my guts? One day when you *really* get to know me, you'll discover I don't intimidate easily.'

'Most cops in Belfast would like to see you dead. They think you've got away with murder in the past, as well as involvement in the killings of police.'

'So, what are you doing sitting with me, if that's what most cops think?'

'One day when you *really* get to know me, you'll discover I'm not most cops. I keep an open mind until I've convinced myself.'

'Fair enough. Anything on Francis' murder?'

'Not yet. We can only stretch manpower so far. If anything comes my way, I'll let you know. Now, you said on the phone you had information for me. I take it you mean Butler?'

'Not that arse-hole. Something important. Do you remember a fire some weeks ago, the entire family were reportedly killed?'

'North Belfast, wasn't it? The Reilly family?'

'Mother, father and two young girls. The young mother's parents–Tommy and Theresa Naughton–asked me to investigate the fire.'

'Why?'

'They weren't too happy with the official findings stating it was an accident, one waiting to happened.'

'And what did you find?'

'Everything the coroner reported was more or less correct. I found nothing suspicious.'

'So, why've you called me if you found nothing to contradict the official report?'

'I found nothing suspicious–*at the time*. It turned out, I was mistaken.'

'That must be a first, coming from you.'

Mary returned with coffee. Conversation recommenced once she left.

'Just like me, the coroner *was* wrong. The fire didn't start accidentally. It was deliberate. Cold-blooded and deliberate.'

'What makes you think that?'

From his coat pocket, Karl removed the disc enclosed in a paper sleeve.

'Thank the gods Tommy and Theresa's perseverance and belief paid off. I just had this made. When you watch it, you'll see that one of the little girls didn't die in the fire. She was abducted.'

'Abducted?' Chambers, looking sceptical, took the disc from Karl. 'You're telling me this disc will show an actual abduction of a young girl?'

'*And* the abductor.'

'You won't blame me for remaining unconvinced, until I look at this?'

'Not at all. I was a Doubting Thomas, until I saw it with my own eyes. But promise me you'll get an alert out immediately after you watch it.'

'I'll have to look at this very carefully before determining what action to take.'

'Don't start with all that bureaucratic bullshit. I wouldn't have come to you if I thought for one moment you'd start talking that shite like all the rest of them. I could have gone to the papers with this, made the cops out to be a right bunch of wankers.'

'Why me? Why'd you want me to have it?'

'Going against my natural instinct, I'm inclined to believe you could actually be the real thing, an oddity, a straight cop. A *good* cop, even.'

'That's a compliment?'

'Save this little girl. Put every resource you have into finding her.'

'You believe she's still alive, even after all this time?'

'What I think doesn't matter. It's what you *do* after you've watch the disc. Apart from doing the right thing, this will be a feather in your cap towards promotion.'

'And will make me eternally grateful to you, of course.'

'You're a very cynical person. Anyone ever tell you that?'

Chambers looked at Karl, then the disc, before pocketing it. Karl sipped on the coffee, and stood to leave.

'You're leaving?'

'I have to be careful about being seen talking to cops. Might make some of my clients nervous. Don't forget to keep me posted on any developments in both cases. I have two brave grandparents waiting anxiously.'

'You're an enigma, Kane. I still haven't figured which category you fall into.'

'Good guy, bad guy?'

'That's right. And just to make it clear: I do everything above board. What I don't do is *quid pro quo*.'

'That's your prerogative. Oh, and talking of quid, pay the bill, and leave a good tip for Mary, like a pro. Take it out of that ten quid you still owe me.'

Karl headed out the door, feeling not only Chambers' eyes following him right out into the street, but the eyes of other cops.

Almost an hour later, Karl turned on to Hill Street, heading for home, carrying blueberry muffins and freshly-brewed coffee from Clements. An early morning treat for Naomi.

As he was about to cross the road towards his apartment, a man brushed against him, almost knocking the bag of pastries and coffee from Karl's hand.

The man turned, looked intently at Karl, as if awaiting an apology.

'That's all right, mate,' Karl said, half smiling. 'You weren't watching where you were...'

Karl stared at the man. Tall. Heavy set. A large deep scar, running from either side of his face, forming a craggy 'Z' all the way to the chin.

The man walked on, no response coming from his lips.

In an instant, Karl found breathing difficult. The street was swooning, in grey, concrete waves. He tried to move. Impossible. Paralysis. The waves began swallowing him. The bag of coffee and muffins slipped from his hands, bursting onto the pavement.

An elderly lady, aided by a cane, approached, concern on her face. 'You okay, son?'

'Huh...?'

'I said, are you okay? You look faint.'

Karl's glance shot up and down the street. Man with scar gone. Was he ever there?

'Come along,' the elderly lady said, taking Karl's arm and pointing her cane at a family of chairs outside a café. 'We'll sit down here for a moment, and you can catch your breath. I'll get you a nice cup of tea.'

'It's...it's okay. I live just across the street. Thank...thank you. I appreciate your kindness.'

The lady kept her eyes on Karl, watching him shakily cross the narrow road and head towards Hill Street.

Inside the apartment, Karl went straight to a wardrobe in the spare bedroom. Opened it. Fished out the pill box from beneath a tower of books and magazines. Slipped three of the pills into his hand, before putting everything back in the wardrobe. Headed into the living room. From a small drinking cabinet, he extracted a bottle of Hennessy and a glass. Filled the glass to the brim. Popped the three pills down his neck, followed by the brandy, all in one swallow. Began pouring another brandy just as Naomi showed up at the door, her angry face on, arms folded tightly.

'Karl, what are you up to, drinking this early? What... what's wrong? What's happened?'

Karl quickly took a slug of the brandy. Sat down heavily on the sofa. Tried steadying shaking hands.

'I...think I just bumped into Walter Arnold – literally.'

'What...?' Naomi's face registered shock and horror. She sat down beside him. 'But...he's in prison. Are you sure it was him?'

'It...*looked* like him. It happened so fast. This guy's face was badly scarred. Arnold's face was scarred just the same way, from an attack in prison, years ago. I think I saw him a couple of weeks ago, too, when I was at the Naughton home.'

Chapter Thirty-Six

'What...? Are you certain?'

'It's only coming back to me now. I didn't get a good enough look at him then. Wasn't positive. He's obviously been tailing me, everywhere I go.'

Naomi didn't look too convinced.

'You've been under so much stress lately, then all the nightmares, Karl. Perhaps...'

'Perhaps what? Perhaps I'm seeing things? Perhaps I'm flying over the cuckoo's nest?'

'I'm sorry. I didn't mean to imply that. Just that it's so strange. One minute we're talking about him; the next thing we know, he appears out of thin air, popping up everywhere. Karl, why don't you call the parole people? Find out if he's been released? That would help ease your mind.'

'I was going to do that, but I'm almost dreading the thought of what they might say. I may not like the answer.'

'You've got to find out, just for your own...' Naomi's voice trailed off.

'Sanity?'

'Of course not. "Peace of mind" is what I was going to say.'

Karl fished the mobile from his pocket. Looked at it for a few seconds, before hitting CONTACT NUMBERS. Parole Board NI. Pressed the button. Silence, then dial tone. A voice on the other end.

'Parole Board of Northern Ireland. David Brown speaking. How may I help?'

'Hello, David. My name is Karl Kane. I'm a private investigator, and I need some information.'

'What kind of information, Mister Kane?'

'I want to know if a murderer by the name of Walter Arnold has been released from prison.'

'I'm sorry, we can't give out that information to the general public.'

'Walter Arnold. You've heard of him?'

'I'm sorry, unless you're the–'

'Shut up and listen!'

'Sir, I don't care for the way you're talking to–'

'Walter Arnold murdered my mother.'

David went quiet for a few seconds. When he talked again, his voice was very low.

'I'm...I'm very sorry to hear that, Mister Kane.'

'I don't want your sympathy, David, just information. Arnold also murdered two young girls, Ann Mullan and Leona Fredrick, both eight years of age. That was after he raped and brutalised them for two days. Then he cut them up for fun. Are you sorry to hear that also, David?'

'I...I can't help you, Mister Kane. Policy clearly states–'

'Stuff your damn policy!' Karl clicked off the mobile. Threw it onto the sofa.

'What did he say, Karl?'

'Nothing. The usual bullshit line about confidentiality. In all honesty, I shouldn't have taken it out on him. He's only doing his damn job. God, I've used that confidentiality bullshit too, when it suited.'

Naomi eased herself up from the sofa.

'Let me get you another brandy.'

'No, it's okay. The moment has gone. I'm fine now. I've got to think. If I can just get some—'

He was interrupted by the loud bleat of his mobile. Reached over and grabbed it. Unfamiliar number. Answered it.

'Hello?'

'Mister Kane? David Brown. Look, I'm sorry about all that. I couldn't talk to you on the work phone, because they monitor our calls, so I took a ten-minute break. It's okay. This is my mobile.'

'Thank you, David. Very much appreciated.'

'According to records, Arnold was released over a year ago.'

'A year ago…why the hell wasn't I informed?'

'I don't know. That's all I can tell you, from what's in his file on the system.'

'Has he an address? A halfway house? Anything?'

'That's higher-level information. I'm just part-time. I'm not privy to that sort of information. Sorry.'

'Nothing to be sorry about, David. I appreciate you sticking your neck on the line.'

'I've got to get back. You…you won't say a thing about this conversation, will you? I'd get the boot, and probably end up in court into the bargain.'

'If you knew me, David, you wouldn't ask that. Rest assured, I never screw people who do me a good turn. If you're ever in need of something, and I mean *ever*, you've now got my number. Okay?'

'Okay. Take care – oh, and good luck.'

Karl clicked off the phone. Looked at Naomi.

'It *was* Arnold. Had to be. The Parole Board bastards released him over a year ago. They were supposed to inform me of any decisions made about the scumbag. That was the deal in court, all those years ago.'

'Don't let them upset you. They're not worth it, the incompetent clowns.'

'I'm not upset, love. I'm *angry*. If Arnold thinks he can stalk me without consequences, he's in for the shock of his scumbag life. And as for the Parole Board? They're going to get both barrels rammed up their arse.'

Chapter Thirty-Seven

*Seek not to know who said this or that, but take
note of what has been said.*
Thomas à Kempis, *De Imitatione Christi*

Early next morning, Karl strode through the doors of the Parole Board headquarters, calmly but with a storm-warning brewing in his eyes. Walking up to the empty counter, he spotted a middle-aged man at a desk working at a computer.

'Excuse me, can you tell me who's in charge?' Karl called to him.

The man's eyes went from keyboard to Karl. He wore a look of hostile disdain, as if looking at a newly released prisoner. After a few deliberate seconds, he got up from behind the computer and walked to the counter. On his shirt was a nam-etag: Peter McCabe.

'Who's asking?'

Karl pulled out a business card. Placed it on the counter. McCabe barely glanced at the card.

'The name's Karl Kane.'

'Have you an appointment?'

'No, Peter. I'm sorry, I don't. But what I do have is a very good friend, sitting outside in my car. He happens to be a brilliant criminal lawyer, and he wants to know why you have released Walter Arnold, a notorious rapist and murderer of children.'

Peter looked as if he had just soiled his pants, and not with soil.

'I...I...I'm not really in charge, per se. That...that would be Mister Hamilton.'

Karl pointed at a blue door.

'For your sake, when I ask you where's Mister Hamilton, you better say he's behind that blue door with the Head Office sign on it. Where's Mister Hamilton, Peter?'

Peter quickly did a Judas, pointing accusingly. 'He's behind that blue door with the Head Office sign on it.'

Karl double-stepped over to the door. Opened it without knocking. Entered, slamming the door loudly behind him.

In his late forties, shirt-and-tie man Hamilton sat at a large mahogany desk, feet naked, beheading lethal-looking dirty toenails with a pair of ancient nail-clippers. His face registered both confusion and shock at seeing Karl. He quickly removed socks and toenail shrapnel from the top of the desk, doing his best to hide the horrid filthy feet.

Karl walked up to the desk, brought his face close to Hamilton's.

'You're Hamilton, I take it?'

'Who...? What are you doing, walking in here unannounced? Who...who gave you permission?'

'Julia Kane, Ann Mullan and Leona Fredrick, to name a few.'

'What on Earth are you talking about?'

'Why did you authorise the release of child murderer and rapist Walter Arnold?'

'Who the hell are you?'

'Karl Kane.'

'Well, Mister Kane, I don't know what this is all about, but I'll give you two seconds to get out of my office and the building, otherwise I'll call the police.'

Karl reached over and grabbed the phone's receiver. Offered it to Hamilton.

'Here you go. I need all the publicity I can get for tonight's news. Arnold raped and murdered my mother, not that you give a damn, of course. So go ahead. Make the call. Let's see what your bosses think when they see the public's reaction to my arrest.'

Hamilton looked at the large hand strangling the receiver. Then up to Karl, who looked like he'd rather be strangling Hamilton.

'I'm...I'm sorry, Mister Kane. I didn't realise who you were, or your circumstances. What exactly is it you want?'

'I want justice, Mister Hamilton. Can you give it to me?'

'How?'

'Why was I not informed of the scumbag's release? It was a part of the court agreement.'

Hamilton gave life to his computer. The screen brightened. His fingers began dancing on the keyboard.

'Here we are. According to this, your family *was* informed, last year, just before Arnold was due to be released.'

'Bollocks! That's a load of shite. Let me see where it says that.'

Hamilton swivelled the computer monitor, so that Karl could see the official letter from the Parole Board. Karl read the letter quickly, going to the name the letter had been sent to.

'Fuck! I don't believe this…'

'I'm sorry, Mister Kane, but it's all there in black and white. As you can see, we did comply with the court agreement,' said a clearly relieved Mister Hamilton.

'The letter was sent to my father, Cornelius.'

'That's right. Head of the family, as required by law.'

'If you dickheads had done your homework, you'd have discovered that address is the address of a nursing home on the outskirts of the city. My father suffers from Alzheimer's. How the hell would you have expected him to read, never mind *understand*, a complex letter like this?'

Hamilton remained silent.

'Can you give me a copy?'

'Certainly. Of course…' Hamilton hit the 'print' button on

the screen, and practically jumped out of his seat, running to the printer at the other end of the room.

Karl watched the printer tonguing the letter out. His stomach began heaving. He wanted to throw up.

'I…I'm really sorry about this terrible mix-up, Mister Kane.'

'You don't get off that easy. Damn you all to Hell,' Karl said with forced calmness, turning his back on Hamilton and walking out the door.

Chapter Thirty-Eight

You're not the only one that had an unhappy childhood,
there are millions like you, and, in my eyes, they are the tough
ones, not you!
Louise (Janine Darcey), *Rififi*

'**A**ny mail addressed to my father, Elaine, how is it
dealt with?' Karl sat across from Elaine Trimble in
her office. Elaine, in her forties and General Manager of the
care home where Cornelius Kane resided, looked every bit the
head nurse she had once been, a no-nonsense, kick-you-in-
the-balls-if-you-mess-with-me-mister sort of woman.

'In all his years living here, Cornelius has read all his own
mail, Karl. That's his right. Quite adamant when it comes to
his privacy. He says it keeps "nosey bastards" like me from
knowing his affairs.' Elaine smiled. As did Karl.

'What if an important letter arrives, one he may not fully
comprehend? What happens then?'

'Actually, we've been seeking legal advice on that very question for all our residents. We've had a few incidents that could
have been avoided if we'd had permission to check certain
residents' mail. We could have saved them a lot of bother

down the road. It's very thin ice. Our residents' dignity is our number one concern, and we have to be careful not to leave ourselves open to lawsuits concerning abuse of trust or invasion of privacy.'

'Do you think Cornelius would have understood any correspondence he received, say, about a year or so ago?'

'A year ago?' Elaine paused to think back. 'Most definitely. Even up to last month, he had no problems reading his mail.'

'Last month…? How do you know?'

'Because I remember the card you sent him on his birthday, with the cheque inside for almost two hundred pounds, and a letter. He was able to tell me everything you wrote, word for word.'

'Does he talk to you much, or to any member of staff?'

'Well, I like to do the rounds each time I'm on duty, see how the residents are doing. Cornelius, as you know yourself, is a man of very few words. He's cordial, most of the time… but sometimes…well, he has his moods. I think he fears the Alzheimer's. It's making him angry, frustrating him. We've had numerous consultations with him, trying to ease his concerns, but it's hard to say if he's blocking out our advice.'

'Would there be any particular staff member he gets on with better than others?'

'Not that I'm aware of. He gets on fine with all the staff, when he's in a good mood. Why do you ask?'

'Just thinking, he may have confided certain things to them.'

'What kind of things?'

'Oh, nothing specific…'

'I can ask around if you like?'

'No, it's okay.' Karl stood to leave. 'Thanks, Elaine. You've been a great help.'

'Are you sure you don't want some coffee before you go in to see Cornelius? You look tired. A caffeine boost might help.'

'No, you're okay. I'll probably make some in his room for the both of us.'

Karl exited, following the snaking corridor all the way to the end, before making a left in the direction of the residents' rooms.

At door 5B, Karl stopped, took a deep breath, rapped, and then entered the room without being invited to do so.

Cornelius Kane was standing, looking out the window. He was tall, but now a desiccated husk of a man, whose only flesh was prominent on the neck in small, saggy accordions of skin.

'Okay, Dad? How's things?'

A Radio Four play filled the room with mellow accents. Cornelius had yet to direct his attention towards Karl.

'What's the play?' Karl asked, removing bars of chocolates and cigarettes from a grocery bag and spilling them on to the bare table. 'Sounds like an Agatha Christie. *The Mousetrap*?'

Cornelius regarded Karl as if seeing a stranger, then set his eyes suspiciously on the goodies spread out across the table.

'What's the trick, Mister? What're you selling? Whatever it is, I'm not buying.'

'No tricks, Dad. I just thought you'd like some of your favourites.'

'You don't look like you're from the Salvation Army, and you sure as hell don't look like Santa Claus.'

Karl laughed. 'You got that right, Dad. It's me, Karl.'

'Karl? Who the hell's Karl?'

The question hit Karl hard, but he tried to disguise any emotion.

'How've they been treating you?'

'You a doctor?'

'No.'

'Then mind your own damn business, Mister. Hand me one of those bars of chocolate.'

Karl picked up one of the Mars bars from the table, and handed it over.

Cornelius studied the wrapper. 'How did you know I only eat Mars bars?'

Karl smiled. 'A guess.'

'A damn good guess, if you ask me. Just who the hell *are* you?'

'I'm your son. Karl. Don't you remember, Dad?'

'You're sick. I'm not your da, and stop calling me it.'

'Okay. Cornelius. How's that?'

'How the hell do you know my name? What's your game? Are you after my money?'

'No…Cornelius,' Karl said, struggling to master his emotions. This giant of a man, once filled with humour and incisive intelligence, was now reduced to the bare bones of his former self, fumbling over rudimentary communications. 'I need to ask you some questions.'

'I knew it the minute you walked into the room, that crafty grin on your ugly gob! You're from the tax people, aren't you? Here to take more money from me. Well, I can tell you now, you'll get none of my money. No, sir!'

Cornelius was becoming visibly agitated. He began to pace up and down the small room.

'Please, Dad – Cornelius. Don't upset yourself. I'm not here to take your money. Just to ask a few questions.' Karl pulled an envelope from the inside of his coat. 'This is a copy of a letter sent to you by the Parole Board over a year ago. Can you remember receiving the original letter?'

'None of your damn business what I read and what I don't.'

'The letter concerns the release of Walter Arnold. You remember him, the monster who murdered your wife and left your son for dead?'

'I don't have a wife or son. Hand me those cigarettes.'

'Not until you answer my questions.'

'You cheeky bastard!' Cornelius pushed Karl away from him, and made an attempt to grab the cigarettes from the table.

Karl gripped Cornelius' hand, hating himself. 'I want answers. Arnold murdered two little girls as well. Remember?

Chapter Thirty-Eight

Ann Mullin and Leona Fredrick. Both aged eight. Raped, then murdered.'

'Give me my cigarettes, you bastard!'

Karl gripped the frail hand tighter. 'Why didn't you contact me, and tell me Arnold had been released? He's been out a whole year. Do you realise what he might have done in that year?'

'Bastard! Nurse! Help! Help!'

'I'm not bloody leaving until I get an answer, so shout all you want. Why didn't you tell me?'

'Nuuuuuuuurse!'

'I know you weren't at sea the night Mum was murdered. You were staying with Martha Johnson, your lover. Weren't you?'

Cornelius looked as if a dagger had been jammed under his chin. He stood stock-still, in shock, before regaining his composure.

'You…you murdered her, not me. Not me…'

'Arnold murdered Mum. Not me. Not you. It wasn't your fault. All this guilt. You've got to talk about it, Dad, before it—'

'Get out of here! Get the hell ouuuuuuut!'

The door opened. Brian, a burly male nurse, ran towards Karl and Cornelius.

'Cornelius! What on Earth's going on?'

'This bastard's attacking me! Tried to steal my cigarettes and my Mars bars, because I didn't let him have one.'

'No one's attacking you, Dad. Calm the hell down, and answer my question.'

Struggling, Brian finally managed to shoehorn himself between Karl and Cornelius.

'Please, Mister Kane,' Brian said, looking at Karl. 'I'm sorry, but I must ask you to leave. Can't you see you're upsetting your father?'

'What the hell are you blabbering about, you nitwit?' Cornelius shouted. '*I'm* Mister Kane. Not that scallywag. And I'm not his father! I don't even know him! Get the police. Have him arrested. He assaulted me!'

'You can blame yourself all you want for Mum's murder, Dad, all those years ago, but you can't close yourself out from the present.'

'*Please*, Mister Kane,' Brian pleaded with Karl. 'I don't want to push the panic button and have you escorted out by other staff members.'

Karl shoved Brian out of the way. 'Don't worry, I'm leaving.' He stopped and pointed a finger at Cornelius. 'I'll be back, Dad. One way or another, you're going to answer the questions I should have asked a long time ago. I *will* get answers.'

Chapter Thirty-Nine

All you need is twenty seconds of insane courage and I promise
you something great will come of it.
Benjamin Mee, *We Bought a Zoo*

Scarman pulled back the bolt to the girls' room, opened the door and walked in. He stood, not saying a word, his breath steaming in clouds.

Dorothy sat huddled on the mattress, head down deep in her chest, legs pulled up tight against her chin, eyes tightly closed. Porcelain, barely breathing, praying silently, asking a deaf god to forgive all her sins. She would never sin again if only he let her go home.

In contrast, Tara stood defiantly in the middle of the floor, legs akimbo, arms resting on her hips. She seemed to have made herself larger than her tiny frame actually was.

Scarman walked beyond her, over to the window. He slowly studied it, running a callused hand along the frame and bars, as if checking for dust. Or something else. He bent on one knee, and held that position for the longest time before standing and heading back towards the door.

'Someone has been leaving this room, and going downstairs,'

he stated in a matter-of-fact voice, bland and flat as a mortuary slab. 'I had a…visitor staying with me. Someone paid him a visit, yesterday, and made him unwelcome. *Very* unwelcome. I don't tolerate rudeness, especially rudeness directed against my guests.'

It was the first time Dorothy had heard him speak. It made her skin feel as if stinging nettles had been inserted underneath. She prayed he didn't notice her shuddering.

'It cannot go unpunished,' he continued in his stoic monotone, glancing from Dorothy to Tara and back. 'Well, which of you is leaving the room? More importantly, how?'

Neither girl spoke. Nor moved.

'Perhaps both of you? Very well, if that's the case…' He lifted Dorothy by the scruff of her neck, before grabbing her ankle and inverting her. 'You'll do for now, little Dorothy.'

'*Noooooooooooooooooooooooooooooooooo!*' Dorothy flayed about, kicking out with her free leg.

Scarman held her at arm's length, fumbling to insert a key into the ankle's manacle. He was finding it difficult.

'Leave her alone, you filthy bastard!' shouted Tara, leaping at Scarman, her fingernails aimed at his smirking face.

With a backhand, Scarman sent her careering to the ground, like a fly being swatted.

'I'll come back for you, after I've enjoyed your little friend.'

'*Noooooooooooooooooooooooooooooooooo!*' Dorothy continued kicking and screaming. *'Don't let him take me, Tara!'*

'Leave her alone. Take me. Take me…' said Tara, rubbing the side of her bruised face. 'It's me you really want, anyway.'

'I've already had you, little whore. I can take you any time I wish.'

'No…no, you haven't, not the real me. I fought you the last time. This time…this time I'll not struggle. I'll do things for you, things you can only imagine.' Tara smiled. Angelic. Her eyes shone. 'Little girl things…things you dream of…wet things…I'll be your good little girl. No-one else can do it like me…you *know* that.'

Scarman stood as if in a daze. Dorothy stopped her struggling and watched his mutilated face. The sweet, melodic sound of Tara's teasing tongue held him in its spell, hypnotising him. He couldn't resist her Pied Piper voice. Gently, almost in slow motion, he lowered Dorothy back on to the mattress.

'If you resist, I'll come back and cut her throat.'

He walked over to unlock Tara's manacle, and only then, too late, did he notice what she was hiding behind her back. The chain seamed itself against her thigh, its manacle free from her ankle, dangling. He looked at it in amazement. Then at Tara.

'*Fuckerrrrrrrrrrrrrrrrrrrrrrrrrrrrrrr!*' Tara put every ounce of fury and hatred into swinging the leash, catching him under the chin, knocking him back against the far wall. She swung and hit him again, this time across the back of the head, and he crumpled onto his knees, dazed and confused.

Removing the razor from the waistband of her jeans, Tara aimed wildly at Scarman's face, slicing off an ear and part of his cheek.

'*Arghhhhhhhhhhhhhhhhhhhhhhhhhhhhhhhhhhhhhhhh!*' Scarman screamed, as Tara raced through the open door, along the landing and down the stairs, leaping them two and three at a time.

On the last flight of stairs, she lost her footing and tumbled, violently banging her head off the wooden banister. Momentarily dazed, she tried to stand, but her ankle felt wrong. *Shit!*

Battling the pain, she moved towards the front door. The three bolts were firmly in place. She pulled the bottom and middle bolts across from their niches, and then balanced on tippy-toes, stretching to reach the final bolt at the top. Her fingertips touched it; she was tantalisingly close, but it was no use.

'*C'mon! You can do it!*' she hissed through gritted teeth, attempting to stand on the bottom bolt. Despite her best try, she could not gain a proper grip. '*Fuck! Think!*'

Turning, she scampered down the hallway, half-running, half-limping, adrenalin dulling the pain in her ankle. She leapt over the soiled mattresses and other debris littering her pathway.

She stopped outside a room. Entered. Butler's body was still there, pinned in the chair, stiff and unloved, eyes staring out at eternity. The body was in the early stages of bloating. It looked like a giant marshmallow melted at the fire. The sickening, cloying death-stench was everywhere, overpowering.

Tara retched. Removed the razor from her waistband, and began hacking through the leather straps holding the body. Suddenly, the body lurched forward, its dead weight released. A loud, suppressed belch emitted from the throat, directly into Tara's face.

'Disgusting dog,' said Tara, kicking the body violently over, before grabbing the chair and running down the hallway.

A bloodied Scarman stood unsteadily, like a drunk overloaded with cheap booze. He brought his hand gingerly around the side of his head to where the ear had once been. Thick, meaty blood attached itself to his hand, as he tried to stem the flow. The hurting he was feeling was beyond pain, but he contained and controlled it, his eyes narrowing, focussing his hate.

He looked down at the floor. The ear nestled in a beard of blood, like a slice of bread in a bowl of tomato soup. It seemed to grin up at him.

'Little bitch! I'll fucking kill you!' he screamed, staggering out the door and giving chase. He couldn't see clearly, swaying from side to side as he ran down the stairs. On the second floor, he too lost his balance. But unlike Tara, he did not tumble to the relative safely of the bottom of the stairs.

Instead, he went crashing through the wooden banisters, crash-landing his face, ribs and lower body.

'*Argggggggggggggggggggggggggggggggggggg!*'

The last thing he remembered was staring at a chair, toppled over in the hallway, and the front door wide open, allowing a gust of wind to enter and mock him.

Tara was gone and there was nothing he could do.

Chapter Forty

I may not have gone where I intended to go,
but I think I have ended up where I needed to be.
Douglas Adams, *The Long Dark Tea-Time of the Soul*

Karl stood outside Francis' house, in a reflective mood. The countryside silence was a balm to his soul, a welcome break from the constant mêlée of Belfast. All around, smells were targeting his nostrils: damp leaves and tree bark mingled with oil and diseased sacks of seed gone to rot; dried diesel smells from the leakage staining a tractor's side, like a wounded beast.

He imagined he could see Francis, working on the tractor, wiping the sweat of hard work from his brow with a blue-and-white handkerchief, freshly starched by Nora.

For a second, the industrial countryside smells were replaced by home cooking and laughter. He saw Nora rapping on the window, beckoning for Francis to come in for dinner, only be sure to take off those muddy boots before daring to set foot inside.

Karl smiled at the memory. Many's the time, he had been given the same command, before feasting at her table.

'Good people…damn good people…'

He ambled around to the back of the house. Police tape fluttered in the wind like weather kites, marking out a rectangle of muck and weeds. The plastic yellow strands seemed to be reaching out to him, like Sirens whispering doom.

Police had determined that the burglar or burglars had entered through the basement. Karl stood at the remains of the door, examining the shattered boards and wedging. A lot of trouble taken to enter a house.

Karl had acquainted himself over the years with burglars, for numerous reasons. One thing they all had in common was the easy approach. He remembered one old hand, Victor Harris, a master burglar, saying to him, if you need to break sweat to break in, then you're doomed to failure – you will end up breaking everything, including your neck.

He stepped into the basement. Dank. Cemented with the stench of neglect. He hit a light switch. Nothing, the naked light bulb dangling from a wooden beam like a hangman's noose. This was giving him the shits. He quickly moved on and through. Three badly constructed concrete steps ushered him into the heart of the house: the kitchen.

He saw himself sitting there at the table, happily chatting with Francis, never realising what cruelty fate had in store, just a few days later.

'Fucking life…' he muttered angrily, seething at the injustice of it all.

In the living room, the forensic cleaners had done a decent job, but he could clearly see the stain of Francis' last grasp on this earth, engrained into the stinking carpet.

Karl peered around the gloomy room, beating himself up psychologically until he was punch-drunk with guilt, contemplating the what-ifs of life, the could-have, should-have, would-have-been scenarios of missed opportunities; he stood there until he was drained and chastened, and a modicum of redemption entered his battered spirit.

Darkness had fallen. Almost two hours had slipped by, unaccounted for. The strange coldness in the room enveloped him in a wary warning, auguring something he could not quite put his touch on.

He shuddered, and made haste to leave, going out the front door this time like a guest, instead of out the back like a thief in the night.

As he closed the front door, behind him, a sound, somewhere from the trees and out-of-control growth of bushes and wildness. Crows began cawing a warning. He stiffened. The sound was almost imperceptible to the human ear, unless that ear was trained to discern danger very quickly.

He craned his neck. Stared out into the gloom of night. He could see nothing, but he knew something was there, watching.

He glanced at Francis' Massey Ferguson tractor, over to his far left. Tried to keep his breathing under control. Edged over to the venerable vehicle. Opened the side door, hoping Francis hadn't let him down. Beneath the driving seat, one of the many shotguns scattered throughout his kingdom.

Karl let out all the pent-up breath. Eased the shotgun out from beneath the driver's seat. Checked its metal stomach. Two shells. Two chances. No more. No less.

The shotgun was aged, with better days seen, but despite this, it made him feel good, its oily smell of self-assurance balancing the odds somewhat.

The bushes directly facing him moved slightly. A ripple made by a night breeze? He cocked the weapon. Dropped to the ground behind the tractor's large wheel. Aimed, more in hope than expectation.

Waited.

The bushes suddenly parted. Someone came running at him from the overgrowth to his right.

'Fuck! King, you bastard.' Karl lowered the weapon as King approached, tail wagging enthusiastically. 'Almost blew your damn tail off.'

Nerves gnawed his spine. He felt like puking. He needed to get home. Get a stiff drink before he ended up a stiff.

His mobile shattered the air. He answered it.

'Naomi? What's wrong?'

'You're not here, *that's* what's wrong.' Her voice sounded on edge. 'Where are you? You told me you'd be back shortly. That was hours ago.'

'I'm sorry, love. Lost track of time. I'm finished here at Francis'. Heading to the car right now, as I speak. I'll make it up to you when I get home. How about a nice meal out?'

'I'd much rather have your nice arse *in*.'

'Well, I have a special on at the minute for beautiful women. You can have both. A meal out, *and* my nice arse in.'

She laughed, but there was a nervous quiver of desperation to it.

'Karl?'

'Yes?'

'Come home. Right now. Please. I…I don't know, just some sort of bad feeling's come over me. Like dread…'

'Don't be worrying. Nothing's going to happen. I'll be home soon.'

He blew kisses down the mobile, before disconnecting.

The whole time Karl was on the mobile, King hadn't stopped barking.

'Hungry, boy? Let's go inside, see where Francis keeps your–'

But King was backing away, barking, its head tilting up and down.

'What's wrong, King?'

King turned, and walked back towards the forest, looking over towards Karl at the same time.

Reluctantly, Karl started following. 'If this is to show me where you buried your last bone, King, I can tell you now you'll be in the shit. Big time.'

As Karl moved further into the interwoven maze of hedges and thickets, he realised they were on some sort of unused road. A stream curled itself along the path, bad smell seeping upwards from it. Sewage or something equally unsavoury. Death in its aquatic sediment.

He quickened his pace, trying to keep up with King, all the while ducking and leaning to avoid the menacing thorns and branches. Rain was coming down now, making navigation more difficult.

As he came out into a clearance, a *déjà vu* dread attacked him. There. Staring at him. In defiance and arrogance. Cycles within cycles. Death born of death.

His mobile rang again. This time, Chambers.

'What the hell do you want?'

'The disc you gave me?'

'Don't tell me you clowns lost it?'

'We pulled a few good stills from it, and used facial-recognition software on the person in the Reilly's backyard. We're almost one hundred percent certain it's Walter Arnold.'

An invisible fist rammed itself against Karl's kidneys. He felt dizzy with concern but also acceptance.

'You still there, Kane?'

'Yes…that's brilliant. Well done to all involved. Now you have the target. Get the bastard.'

'We will. We're hoping to catch him off-guard.'

'Where exactly would that be?'

'I suppose I can tell you now without compromising security. Two Greenway Lane, over in the—'

'North of the city…'

'Oh, you're familiar with that part of town? You know the
place?'

'I'm looking at it right now, standing a few feet away.'

'What? What's that supposed to mean?'

'It's where I used to live…' Karl said, much too calmly.

'Kane, don't. Don't go in there. For your own safety.'

'Concerned about my safety? Very touching, Chambers.'

'Don't be doing this, Kane. I know how you must be feeling, what you want to do, but—'

'I can't hear you. You're breaking up. Bad reception, up here
in the hills.'

'Kane! For Heaven's sake, don't be—'

Karl turned off the mobile completely. No more calls. No
more voices. No more excuses.

He looked at King. The rain was easing now, and a waning
half-moon cast a theatrical silver sheen over the old house.

'Coming with me, boy?'

King refused to budge, as if sensing something unpleasant
lurking in the building.

'Not as stupid as I look, eh, boy?' Karl said, patting King's
head before moving towards the door.

Chapter Forty-One

Piglet sidled up to Pooh from behind. 'Pooh?' he whispered.
'Yes, Piglet?'
'Nothing,' said Piglet, taking Pooh's hand.
'I just wanted to be sure of you.'
AA Milne, *Winnie-the-Pooh*

The front door was unlocked. Ajar. Karl pushed it open apprehensively with the barrel of the shotgun. There was nervousness in his movements. He felt hollowed out from tension, like he had scraped the bottom of his adrenal glands. He didn't know if he had any more fight, or flight, in him. He peered in. The darkness within was diluted by tiny beads of moonlight, leaking in to expose an upturned chair in the hallway. The blood-soaked chair had dried out in whorls and dark knot patterns. It looked like a left-over from the Turner Prize.

Karl studied the chair with wary puzzlement in his eyes, as his peripheral took in everything else around him.

He stepped inside, as if approaching a landmine. *Breathe, just keep breathing.* The deadly silence was drilling into his ears, as if he was submerged in thick, viscous fluid. The shotgun moved to his left, then to his right, as if waiting for a hail of bullets to come storming out of the darkness.

I've been watching too many fucking movies – and bad ones at that...

Newspaper clippings and snapshots wallpapered every conceivable space. Some of the clippings told of Karl's mother's death; others of the murders of Ann Mullin and Leona Fredrick, and the subsequent trial of Walter Arnold.

Karl recognised himself in quite a few photographs. There were four or five of him entering and leaving the Reilly household. Karl's mind flashed back to that day, to the man standing there with the camera. Shit. If only he had realised, back then.

The house was a coalition of feelings he thought he had long ago excised. Smells were flocking all around him, like feeding seagulls. He could smell damp and aged washing powder, and bleach spillage. It made him think of his mother filling the washing machine with dirty clothes, while he played out in the glorious sun. Her smile. Her voice filling the house. Roots here in his very bloodstream.

Other smells here also. Overwhelming and sinister. He could smell excrement, piss spillage glazed with rotten vegetables, unwashed bodies. But topping this menu of wretchedness was the unique perfume of death.

He didn't want to think negatively, but Dorothy instantly, automatically, sprang to mind.

'Please don't let it be her...please...'

He advanced cagily down the corridor. The stench was more pronounced down here, the darkness more complete. He glanced into the room to his left. Entered.

Karl didn't recognise Butler's corpse initially, but once he saw the carved-up and bloated forearm, he knew. Death in all its brutal nakedness can make hot blood run cold, make one more reflective of past thoughts and deeds.

He pitied Butler, lying on the floor naked, dead and alone, tortured and humiliated and ultimately snuffed out. If someone had told him a few days earlier that he would one day feel sympathy for the crime boss, he would have laughed. Yet, here he was, feeling exactly that.

But why in the hell was Butler here? Had he partnered Arnold, joined forces to snare Karl? Had it all gone awry, for some reason known only to the duo? He wouldn't have pictured Butler – despite his faults – as wallowing in child abduction and abuse. Still, you can't judge a book by its cover. No doubt it would all come out in the wash. Karl hoped he would still be around once that wash was done and the wrongdoers were hung out to dry.

He made his way up the stairs, easing each footstep down gently in the hope of not making too much noise. Even after all these years, he still remembered which wooden steps squeaked, which didn't.

The rain outside was gathering momentum again. The emptiness of the great house multiplied its sound. He could barely hear himself thinking. Then thunder filled the air, unnerving him further. He stopped for a moment, just to steady the boat. Lightning hit the top of the house, sending slates rattling off the roof in a mad stampede.

Instinctively, he ducked his head, as if they were raining down on him. He pointed the shotgun towards the roof.

'*Fucking bastards…*' He laughed nervously.

Lightning struck again, momentarily giving brightness to the suffocating dark. A ghostly figure of a woman looked down at him from the top floor. She seemed to be pointing to the master bedroom, jabbing her finger in an urgent indication. The eerie sight took what little breath he had left.

'*What the…?*' She was attired in her favourite sweater of teapots. '*Mum…*'

The figure disappeared as the gloom settled again.

He blinked a few times, trying to clear his eyes, rally his thoughts. He began to tremble. A heroin addict in the depths of cold turkey. The pills. He needed the damn pills. *Now.* Help to calm the situation. Regain his composure. Help him think straight. Not see ghosts. Not see dead mothers long turned black-boned and empty-eyed.

He took a deep breath. Exhaled. Nice and slowly. Repeated. Let the oxygen go to the brain. It slowed the hammering in his chest a touch.

No ghosts. Only a monster, and you need to slay it before it slays you…

He inched onwards, strangely feeling more confident, but also more reckless. A cold calm began to assert itself. If he was to die, then fuck it. But he wouldn't die until he had killed Arnold, this night, in this house.

Outside the master bedroom, he pushed his back against the wall, and listened. He could hear a sound. Someone hiding in the dark, waiting to ambush him? Is that what the woman was pointing at? He berated himself for such puerile thoughts. No. There was no woman. No mother. Lightning playing tricks. Still…

He brought the shotgun up to his waist. Poked the barrel into the darkness. Placed his finger on the trigger. He would fire one shell into the room, towards the ceiling. From the gun's flash, he would have a microsecond of advantage, might see where the bastard was hiding. The flash would hopefully confuse Arnold as well. That's all the advantage he would have, a microsecond. With the second shell, he would blow Arnold's head clean off his fucking shoulders.

Karl slowly inhaled. He did a countdown in his head.

Three…two…o—

Whimpering. A heart-breaking whimpering.

Karl stopped counting. Brought the shotgun down to his side.

'Who's in there?' he hissed.

The whimpering stopped.

'I said, who the hell's in there?'

Nothing.

'Dorothy? Is that you, Dorothy? Say something to me, love.'

Nothing.

'I...I'm a friend of the family. Your granny and granddad sent me to find you. Theresa and Tommy Naughton. Say something, Dorothy. Please, love.'

Nothing.

Then.

'I'm...in here...please don't hurt me,' a small voice finally sobbed. 'I don't want to be hurt any more. I'm sorry for all the bad things I did. Just don't hurt me...please...'

Karl stepped in. Quickly scanned the room. Dorothy was curled up in the far corner, knees up to her bowed head. It was pitiful to behold. Karl could feel his heart clench into a hard knot, then fill with such anger he silently cursed a god who turned a blind eye to such evil. He quickly knelt beside her. She was shaking.

'It's okay, Dorothy. You're going home. Tiddles is waiting for you.'

Slowly Dorothy brought her head up, daring to peep out over her knees.

Karl was shocked by her scrawny, emaciated appearance. An urchin from a Dickens story. He would never have recognised her from the family portrait. He thought of his beloved Katie. Tears began to form in his eyes. He quickly brushed them away with the sleeve of his coat. Took the coat off and wrapped it around Dorothy's shaking shoulders.

'Tiddles? You…you know our wee Tiddles?'

'I sure do know Tiddles, Dorothy. She's the queen of all cats. She found you. Not me. Tiddles.'

'How? How did she find me?'

'It's a long story, but I've got to get you out of here first, before telling you all about it.'

'Will…will you take me home to my mummy and daddy, and our wee Cindy?'

Karl couldn't look her in the face. Tears were threatening in his eyes again. 'I'm taking you home.'

A feeble smile appeared on Dorothy's face. 'What's…what's your name, Mister?'

'Karl.'

'Karl? Just like my bear.' Dorothy held out the old, mangled teddy bear. In a flash, Karl recognised his bear. Remembered the day his father bought it for him. He forced a smile. Patted the bear's head.

'That's a great bear, Dorothy. Many's the night he helped to get me through the dark. Come on. Time to go…' Only then did he see the chain attached to her tiny ankle. His blood started to rise again. 'You…you've been chained all this time, to this damn wall?'

Dorothy nodded. 'Yes…me and Tara.'

'Tara? Who's Tara?'

'She escaped. Scarman did terrible things to her.'

Chapter Forty-One

'Scarman…?' *Arnold.*

'She pretended to be my friend. Said she was going to take me with her, but she didn't. I hate her now.'

He rested the shotgun against the wall. 'I need you to turn your head away, Dorothy, and close your eyes. Just for a few seconds, in case the dust gets into them. I need to try and pull this chain from the wall. Ready?'

'Okay.' Dorothy turned her head, squeezed her eyes shut. Hugged the bear tightly. 'We're ready.'

Karl wrapped the chain around his wrist twice, then a third time for good measure. He began pulling. Nothing. Attached too firmly to the wall. He gritted his teeth. Pulled. Nothing.

'C'mon! You can do it!' This time he thought of Arnold, of all his degraded, malevolent deeds. The chain became Arnold's neck. Karl pulled again. His face bulged, turning red with pressure. Dust started to tumble from where the chain was esconced. He could see Arnold's smirking face on the wall, laughing at him in defiance. '*Nooooooooooooooooooooooooooooo oooo!*'

A link in the chain snapped, shooting into the air. Karl slipped onto the floor, landing on his arse, winded.

'Karl!' Dorothy shouted, rushing to him. 'Karl! Are you hurt?'

Karl smiled, despite everything. 'My pride, Dorothy. That's all.'

'Look! You did it! The chain snapped. You're Superman!'

'I'll have to remember that in future.' He quickly stood, and scooped her up in his arms. He grabbed the loose chain on her ankle and gathered it up. 'We'll get this off once we get outside. No time to do it here.'

He took the stairs as quickly as he could without tripping over anything, his eyes and ears hunting the darkness for sight or sound.

Outside, the torrential rain was creating tiny nomad streams, passing the side of the house as if trying to flee. King waited. Motionless and soaked. Only when he spotted Karl did the tail wag slightly.

'I thought you were smarter than that, boy.'

'Oh, he's beautiful, Karl. What's his name?' said Dorothy, staring down at the dog.

'King.' He put Dorothy down.

Immediately she started to pat King's head and hug his neck. Karl straightened up to his full height. 'Can you do something for me, Dorothy? Something very important?'

'What?'

'Can you look after King for me, just for a few minutes?'

Dorothy's face suddenly became fearful. 'You…you're leaving me. I don't want to be left alone.'

'You won't be alone. You'll have King. He's a great guard dog.'

Dorothy slowly nodded. 'Okay, but you're coming home too, aren't you?'

Karl smiled. There was a sadness to it. 'Of course I'll be going home...I just need to go inside for a few moments.'

'Okay. I'll look after King. But don't be long.'

He ruffled her hair, then turned and went back inside.

Chapter Forty-Two

It is the desperate wail of the Cicada, surprised in his quietude by the Green Grasshopper, that ardent nocturnal huntress, who springs upon him, grips him in the side, opens and ransacks his abdomen. An orgy of music, followed by butchery.

Jean-Henri Fabre, *The Wonders of Instinct*

Karl slammed the door behind him. Slid the middle bolt into its niche. Tried calming the tiny jumps in his stomach. Took a couple of deep breaths before shouting into the darkness.

'Just you and me now, Arnold! No kids. No women. No little girls to take your evil perversions out on. Man-to-man, though we both know you were never a man to begin with. Just a gutless animal, a spineless–'

'You were in such a hurry to get out, Karl, you forgot something!' The voice called out from above, loud and powerful, but flat, as though incapable of emotion.

An unmerciful clatter of metal landed at Karl's feet. He glanced down.

Sweet fuck! The shotgun. What a clown you really are. You know it's still not too late to turn and run. Do something smart for a change. Think of those who love you – Katie, Naomi. They don't want a dead hero. They want you back in their arms.

'I suppose you've taken out the shells, Arnold?'

'Why don't you pick it up and see for yourself? I'm not an unsporting person.'

The darkness seemed to become denser the longer Karl stood there, debating with himself. He looked down at the shotgun, as though he could determine whether it was still loaded – any indication, no matter how flawed. It looked loaded. It looked empty.

'Who's the coward now, Karl, standing there shitting yourself, instead of grabbing the weapon? All of your brave talk is nothing but vanity and chasing after wind. Even that smelly farmer gave more of a fight, before I blasted his fat belly all over the wall. Took him an hour to die, you know. I had a meal in his kitchen while I watched him squirm and twitch.'

Karl buckled his knees, fell onto his shoulder, scooping up the shotgun, and rolled for shelter beside the staircase's wooden ribs. He waited for his head to be blown into a million pieces of meat, but nothing came.

'Well, Karl? Is it loaded or not?'

Karl checked. It was loaded.

'See? Didn't I tell you I wasn't unsporting? You owe me big time, Karl. Oh, and don't forget, I killed Butler for you. The cheek of him, thinking he was going to take my pleasure away. No one gets to kill you. No one except–'

Kaboom!

Karl fired towards the voice, moving at the same time to the bottom of the staircase, forcing his feet to take the steps two at a time. He flattened his body out on the second floor landing, out of breath, sweating and gagging on air. He was still alive! He wanted to laugh with joy, scream it out at Arnold.

'That was dirty of you, Karl. Missed by a mile, but still, very dirty. It seems that I won't be able to take you alive as I had planned, fuck you in the arse again, the way you loved it, all those years ago.'

Don't let the bastard screw with your mind. Let him talk his way to his own grave.

'No answer, Karl? You mother loved it, getting in the arse. Oh, she dearly *loved* it. I think that's why *you* enjoyed it so much, knowing my cock had been up her arse first. Come on now. Tell the truth, shame the devil.'

Arnold was laughing, but it had a dullness to it.

The bastard is hunched down somewhere, hiding. He's as fucking scared as I am.

Karl crawled along the landing, stopping at the blind spot where the stairs ran into the third floor banisters. The old storage room directly to his left. If he could get in there, it would offer a slight – *very* slight – advantage.

He took the chance, almost breaking his neck in the process. The shotgun hit the side of the door and went spinning out of his hands, down into the abyss.

'Fuck!'

For a few seconds, Karl sat immobile, trying to dream up some new strategy. The old wardrobe mirror, in the far corner of the room, reflected his desperation right back at him through the shadows. He hardly recognised himself. He looked terrified. Lost.

'I hate guns. Too loud. Too vulgar,' said Arnold, standing at the door, holding the shotgun and a serrated hunting knife. He threw the shotgun at Karl's feet. 'Take it. You have one shell left, remember?'

Karl looked at the shotgun. Then at the monster standing before him. Arnold's face was strapped up with silver duct tape, the spaces in between covered in dried blood, his features barely recognisable as human.

'Well? What are you waiting for, Karl? Take it. You get one more chance. Make sure your aim is true and–'

Karl rugby-tackled Arnold. They both went flailing backwards, towards the banisters, crashing through them as though they were mere matchsticks. They went hurtling downwards, each grabbing the other in desperation, as if somehow that would save either of them.

In slow motion, Karl watched his life flash in front of him, as he gripped Arnold's throat.

The sudden impact bounced both men off the mattresses, sending each in a different direction.

'*Argggggggggggggggggggggggggghhhhhhhhhhhhh!*' screamed Karl, both legs snapping instantly upon impact. '*Fuckkkkkkkkkkk-kkkkkkkkkkkkkkkkkkkkkkkkkkk!*'

Arnold fared much better, his upper body cascading off the bottom of the stairs, dulling impact. However, he then landed awkwardly, snapping his left wrist and breaking three fingers. He moaned but, unlike Karl, he did not scream.

Karl felt consciousness leaving him. The blackest ink seemed to be seeping into every part of him. Strangely, he could no longer feel pain, as if he had destroyed that particular barrier and it could no long hold any power over him.

Arnold dragged himself over to Karl, knife in hand. Like Karl, he could barely breath and was taking great gulps of dusty air into his lungs, making him cough and splutter. He placed the knife under Karl's throat.

Arnold seemed to be saying things, but Karl only saw a mouth moving in soundless syllables. His eyelids were becoming heavier and heavier, his will to live and fight quickly ebbing away.

Behind Arnold, someone appeared. A girl? A woman? She was holding a cutthroat razor. She was wearing *that* sweater.

'Mum…?'

She was smiling down at Karl, but not in a nice way. The last thing Karl remembered was warm blood. So much of it. Stinging his eyes. Filling his mouth. He was swallowing it, choking on it…

Hidden in the midst of brambly bushes across from the house, Dorothy watched as a stream of police cars snaked up the hilly path. Some of the cars were having difficulty navigating the mucky road.

'Look, King. We're safe now. Here come the police.'

King wagged its tail, but kept its eyes trained on the front door.

'I know, King. I wish Karl would hurry up too. I wonder what's keeping him?'

Just then, the door opened. A figure stepped out. Covered in blood.

'Tara!' Dorothy ran towards her. Wrapped her arms around her waist. 'You didn't leave me after all!'

Tara hugged her tightly. 'I told you I would never leave you, didn't I?'

'Yes...'

'Now you've got to listen to me, for one last time.'

'Okay.'

'Soon, you'll be home. Home with people that love you.'

'I know, but aren't you coming with me? They'll love you, as well as me.'

'I can't go with you, Dorothy. I've...I have people who love me too. I can't let them down.'

'You're my best friend. You can't leave me.'

'Listen, I don't have much time. Do you really love me, Dorothy? I mean, *really* love me?'

'Yes! You know I do, Tara.'

'They're going to ask you questions about me.'

'Who, Tara? Who's going to ask me questions?'

'Everyone. The police, newspapers, your family. You mustn't tell them anything. Do you understand? I would be in trouble if you do.'

'Trouble? What kind of trouble?'

'Big, big trouble. They'd put me back in Blackmore for ever and ever. They'd beat me every night. Do bad things to me. Is that what you want?'

'No! I won't let them take you away. I won't!'

'Then you mustn't tell them anything.'

'I…I won't, Tara. I won't.'

'Promise?'

'I promise.'

Tara gave Dorothy a long hug, and then kissed her cheek.

'I'll always be watching over you, Dorothy. Never forget that.'

Dorothy watched Tara disappearing into the forest, the rain following behind her like a giant cloak of darkness. She watched until there was nothing more to watch, and then she began sobbing.

Chapter Forty-Three

*You either die a hero, or you live long
enough to see yourself become the victim.*
Harvey Dent, *The Dark Knight*

Two days went by before Karl was able to receive visitors at the hospital. Both broken legs were in stirrups, with plaster of Paris encasing his entire lower half. His ribs hurt like hell, as did parts of his spine. His face looked a mess, but in a ruggedly handsome, tough-guy sort of way. Ironically, it was his birthday. He was feeling sorry for himself, but did his best not to show it.

First in the long line of visitors were his beloved daughter Katie, and not so beloved ex-wife Lynne. He was quite surprised to see Lynne, though he knew it was probably through Katie's pressure rather than any sense of sentimentality from Lynne.

'Happy birthday, Dad!' Katie hugged and kissed him, before setting a birthday card on the table, alongside a large bottle of Lucozade.

'You've not come bearing gifts of chocolates, fruit or flowers?' he asked Lynne, as she sat down behind Katie, well away from the bed.

'If I remember correctly, you're allergic to flowers and choc-olate. And I'm not going to make these young nurses' lives more miserable by bringing fruit. Can you imagine the state of your bedpan?'

'Yes, you're right. How inconsiderate of me to want to take a shit.'

'Mum? Dad? Can we stop the squabbling for a few min-utes?' said Katie, getting no response from either parent.

Katie could do nothing but cry once she took in the extent of Karl's injuries, no matter how many times Karl lied that the broken bones and messed-up face were all superficial.

He was more than a little suspicious about Lynne's attitude, though. At times, she showed some sympathy for his injuries; but there were a few times he thought he could detect a hint of gloating in her voice. Perhaps a broken neck would have been more up her street? Despite himself, he had to smile when she said, 'It could have been worse; could have been a broken dick.' He wanted to, but didn't, respond that she would prob-ably know more about broken dicks than he.

Katie signed the plaster cast, but Lynne ignored it, stating she 'didn't do that sort of thing'.

No sooner had Katie and Lynne left, than in walked Detec-tive Chambers, also bearing no gifts of comfort.

'Not even a grape? Are all cops such tight-arse cheap bas-tards? How the hell can you come to hospital and not bring something with you?'

Chambers looked embarrassed. 'I…I just never thought.'

'That's the problem with people nowadays. Anyway, hurry the hell up with whatever questions you have. I've real people coming to see me in fifteen minutes.'

'I'll be as quick as I can. May I sit down?'

'Just don't get too comfortable. I think I may have to use the bedpan very shortly.'

'Thank you.' Chambers pulled a chair close to the bed. Sat down. 'How are you doing?'

'Are you for real? I've a bedpan under my arse and I'm pissing down a straw. Want to ask any more stupid questions?'

'Sorry. Wasn't thinking.'

'I hope you understand, I don't have to give you an interview. I'm only doing it out of the kindness of my heart and civil duty.'

'I fully understand that, and appreciate it, especially after what you went through,' said Chambers, pulling out a notepad, and flicking through a few pages. 'Any idea what Butler was doing at the house?'

'Didn't you ask him?'

'Can we conduct this without levity, please? People died back there, regardless of what they may or may not have done.'

'Really? Did you see what that bastard Arnold did to that little girl, Dorothy Reilly? No may-or-may-not bullshit. So you don't get to tell me not to laugh at him. Fuck him.

Rot in hell. Now, hurry up with your next bloody question, before I have you kicked out on your arse.'

Flustered, Chambers flicked a page, quickly studied his notes. 'This mysterious figure you were talking incoherently about, in the ambulance? According to you, she came out of nowhere, and she saved your life by cutting Arnold's throat?'

'I was in a state of shock, so I really can't remember much about what I supposedly said in the ambulance. Can't even remember the ambulance, to be frank. *Okay?*'

'Of course. I fully understand that. I'm just trying to clear up as much of this as I can, for the record.'

'For the record? If I tell you anything, it's *off* the record. Understood?'

Chambers was hesitant, unsure. Finally he said, 'Okay, provided it doesn't incriminate me down the line. And don't ask me to withhold evidence.'

'It was my mother.'

'Your mother…?'

'The mysterious figure. I know it sound nuts, but it's the truth. Don't ask me how, but it was. Thank God she was there; otherwise I wouldn't be here, and neither would you.'

Chambers studied Karl, a man with concussion, a man traumatised beyond understanding, doped to the eyeballs on morphine and God-alone-knew-what-else he himself might have added to the mix. A man who lived perpetually outside the sphere of normal people's understanding and thinking about this world.

'I'll leave you now.' Chambers stood. 'I think I have enough for my boss.'

'Wilson? The bastard's back from Edinburgh?'

'Yesterday.'

'What did he say when he learned of my misfortune? Bet he couldn't stop laughing?'

'I wasn't the one who informed him, so I'm not privy to what he actually said. However, I have heard from a reliable source that he seemed…uplifted…'

'Uplifted? Yes, that would be him all right, the bastard. You just watch your back, with him. He's a natural liar, whose tongue could fry an egg. Tell him if he wishes to come visit, I've a bedpan needs emptying.'

Chambers low-laughed. 'I doubt I'll pass that particular request on to him.'

'Before you go – what about Dorothy? Any news of her?'

'She's in a children's ward in this hospital. They're keeping her there for observation. They haven't told her yet about her parents and younger sister.'

Karl shook his head, a huge weight of sadness in his voice. 'Puts everything into perspective, doesn't it? I'm lying here, moaning about not being able to take a leak, and that child has yet to be told of the nightmare awaiting her. Doesn't seem right, does it?'

'No. It doesn't.' Chambers turned to leave, but stopped. Held out his hand. 'I...we all appreciate what you did, rescuing Dorothy. It was very courageous.'

'Well, you could have shown your bloody appreciation a little more clearly by bringing something with you, something in liquid form.'

'You're right. I should have. Tell you what I'll do. I'll pick something up and leave it at reception for you, later. How's that sound?'

Karl finally shook the hand. 'Make it a large bottle of Hennessy, but don't leave it at reception, in case it grows legs and disappears. Leave it at my office. No, forget that. Naomi's on her own. Leave it till next week, when I can be there to keep a close eye on you. Good day, Detective Chambers.'

Finally, in walked Naomi, looking as if she hadn't slept in a very long time. She burst into tears the moment she set eyes on Karl, on the ruined state of his body. Ran to him. Hugged him tightly, before kissing his wounded face over and over again.

'Oh, my poor Karl! What have they done to you?' She held him for so long, he eventually had to lever himself out of her grip.

'I should break my legs more often if this is the outcome.'

She giggled nervously. Brushed away the tears. Laughed some more. Tears returned.

'I don't want to say happy birthday, under the circumstances, but happy birthday, big fella.' She handed him a small, oblong box.

'For me?' Karl said, playing coy while opening the box.

'I know you don't believe in all that religious stuff, but it would make me feel a lot happier to know you have it.'

'Your Saint Christopher medal? But this belonged to your grandmother. I know how much this means to you, Naomi. I can't take it.'

'You can and you will. Anyway, it'll comfort me to know you're wearing it. It'll help keep you safe.'

'Bit bloody late!'

'You know what I mean.'

'Didn't I read somewhere that big Chris was kicked out of the gang, up in Heaven?'

'Will you do this for me, and stop arguing? And don't worry, I've a couple of other presents for you for when I get you home.'

'Do you never stop thinking of sex? To be honest, my cock's a lot stiffer with all this plaster on it. Want to see?'

'At the minute, I'm more interested in other parts of your body. How are your legs?'

'Still attached to my arse, last time I scratched it.'

She laughed, and it was the best medicine Karl had had in two days. Then her laughter turned to tears.

'If anything had happened to you, Karl, I...I don't know what I would've–'

'*Shhhhhhhhh.*' Karl bridged a finger on her lips. 'Let's not talk about it now, love. I'm safe and sound, it's okay, I'm right here.'

Naomi wiped away snot and tears. 'Look at me! I must look such a mess.'

Karl pulled her over to him. 'The kind of mess I love.'

He kissed her, long and lovingly. Tasted the salt from her tears. Felt tears welling in his own eyes. Placed his head on her shoulder, and hugged her tightly.

'I'd die without you, Naomi. You know that, don't you? I could never survive.'

She said nothing, but he felt her head nodding on his shoulder; felt her body tremble as more tears came.

'I hope I'm not interrupting something here?' Lipstick, smiling, stepped into the room. 'I rapped on the door, but no answer.'

Naomi pushed away from Karl, wiping her eyes with her sleeve.

'This is the best birthday I could have wished for. All my favourite women in the same room, all within an hour of each other – well, *almost* all my favourite women. Lynne was here too.'

Lipstick hugged Naomi, then walked over to the bed and hugged and kissed Karl. She handed him an expensive-looking watch box.

'Happy birthday, Karl.'

'Lipstick…you shouldn't have,' said Karl, hesitantly taking the box. He knew immediately it was going to be trouble. Sixty thousand quid's worth of trouble. The fact it was a dead man's watch made him uncomfortable. Still, Patek Philippe was not to be sniffed at, truth be told.

He slowly opened the box. The watch stared out at him. He removed it from its enclosure.

'A Timex…? How timely,' said Karl, not knowing if he should be glad or sad.

Lipstick's face lit up. 'You like it, Karl? Really?'

'What's…what's not to like about a Timex…?' Karl said, trying to inject some enthusiasm into his disappointed voice.

'Take a look at the watch's motto, engraved on the back. That's why I bought it. It reminded me so much of you.'

Karl slowly turned the watch over. Read the motto to himself. A large smile spread across his face.

'What's the smile for, Karl?' said Naomi. 'What does it say?'

'It says, *"Timex, it takes a licking but keeps on ticking"*.'

Epilogue

We all end up dead, it's just a question of how and why.
William Wallace

He sat at the window, watching pellets of rain bounce and skid on the tarmac outside the old building. The radio was playing a song from the fifties. It transported his mind back to better days. Good days. Family days. No betrayal. No darkness.

He waited until the song ended, before easing himself from the chair and making his way into the bathroom. There, he reached for a tube of denture cream. Looked at it, as if searching for an answer. Returned to his seat at the window.

Another song came on. He vaguely remembered it. Tried to summon up the singer's name, but the pain in his head blocked all cognitive thought. He found it exhausting.

Flipping the tube over, he began working on the sealed bottom. Not sealed enough. False. It had taken him a couple of days to make it look perfect. He couldn't risk them finding it when they came in cleaning, twice a week.

After twenty laborious minutes, he had finally managed to squeeze out the hidden gems: sixteen sleeping pills concealed within the mushy mess.

They had thought him stupid, but he had outsmarted them all. He could outsmart anyone, when the chips were down. Anyone.

He began to wipe the pills, one by one, getting the gooey mess off them. He had always hated the aftertaste the cream brought after usage. He would never have to worry about that again.

He filled a glass with lukewarm water, and popped one pill in his mouth. Repeated the action, until all sixteen were gone.

After a few minutes of contemplation, he made his way to the bed, and got inside. Made himself comfortable. Removed one of three pillows, and placed it on the floor beside his slippers. His nightly ritual, undisturbed. Prying night eyes would see nothing but routine.

They would find him in the morning, but of course it would be too late – for them, not him. They would make a false fuss, but within a couple of days, he'd be forgotten. He smiled slightly at the thought.

Then he closed his eyes for the last time.

PAST DARKNESS

Across town, Karl was having difficulty sleeping. The pain in his legs seemed to be intensifying, despite the dosage of morphine injected into his system. From the side table, he picked up this evening's newspaper, and reread it for the umpteenth time. His story was still making the headlines. He was a hero. A maverick. Perhaps a mixture of both, with a little added gung-ho-bad-boy thrown into the mix.

Naomi said the phone hadn't stopped ringing, potential and future clients all queueing up for his services. The business might even have to expand, to keep up with demand.

Eventually, his eyelids became heavier. The newspaper slipped from his grasp, fluttering onto the floor like a wounded bird. For some unknown reason, his last thoughts were of his father.

BRANDON